Royally Rugged

J.P. Sterling

Contents

Blurb

Erralee has a decision to make. One choice promises to save lives and end a ruthless war. The other is her one shot at true love.

Erralee D'Long

My fate was stolen the day my arrogant father made a deal to save his country. Now, I've promised to marry a powerful king of a faraway kingdom.

Sounds like a fairy tale, but it is a nightmare.

The only feelings I have for this man is dread, dread, and more dread.

Since I have no desire to be betrothed, I'm running away. Problem solved.

Reeves Mathews

Discharged from the army with a pat on the back and a prosthetic hand, all I want is a fresh start. I'm happy to score the last plot of farmland from the king's recent auction. Excited to get on with my life *alone*, everything is going according to plan until a snowstorm traps the girl next door at my house.

Did I mention she's beautiful?

As hard as I try to fight our connection, I can't deny there's something there.

Oh, yeah, I forgot to say she's also a princess, who is engaged to a king who owns the most powerful army.

Lucky me, right?

***Royally Rugged* is an opposite world, off-limits, forced proximity, modern day fairytale with all the feels.**

**Just Kisses *No Swears * No Blasphemies*

Introduction

Where in the world does this story take place?

I had a few readers confused by the royal theme as it felt very fantasy to them. That was never my intention. I have a daughter in her princess era, which therefore makes me in my *second* princess era, and I'm owning it. I've been asked where this story takes place, and I didn't assign it to any geographic region. If you need to pinpoint somewhere on the map to help you visualize this, we will say this book takes place on an island where *fairy tales are made.*

To Erralee: Thank you for letting me use your beautiful name as inspiration for this story.

One
Reeves

"Private Mathews." Sarg announced his presence from the combat support hospital room doorway. In pristine uniform as always, he stood with his heels clicked together.

"Sargent Darcy." I laid flat on my back without a pillow, aware that something was missing when I went to salute. I couldn't lay here, not showing respect. I fumbled to pull my other hand out from the linen blanket and offered a left-handed salute.

Sarg positioned his hand for salute, holding it in pause. After a long beat, he dropped his hand with his signature, "Very well." As he crossed the room, flashing an envelope in the air, my stomach dropped.

"Discharge papers." I stared at the letter without reaching for it. It wasn't a total shock. Obviously, I couldn't continue to serve with only one hand, but it was not the instant flood of relief I would have assumed I'd feel. It was simply the last punctuation mark on a sentence conveying frustration.

I had planned for a military career my entire child-hood. Playing with green plastic army soldiers in my living room every day. This was something I was born to do. Of course, I enlisted during peacetime, when it was an easy way to travel, and pick up a few foreign languages. All that changed when the country was invaded. After two years of war, and now an amputation, my military career had come to a screeching halt.

"What are you going to do now?" Sarg asked, still holding the letter. It was a bit of an awkward exchange since he was standing closest to my missing hand. For me to grab it, I'd have to sit up and reach all the way across my own body. I didn't have the strength to do that.

"I guess I'll start over." It wasn't hard for me to say that. Actually, it seemed rather nice to say. *New Beginnings.*

"I heard King D'Long is auctioning off some of his private farmland. It sounded like it might be a peaceful place to transition to civilian life."

"Really?" I coaxed my head to the side, visions of rolling prairie flashed through my mind. My grandfather had farmed a bit when I was younger. He was already past retirement age, and mostly just hayed the fields, but I had spent many Saturdays on his lap in the tractor. We'd listen to the only station that came in on the tractor's AM radio, and spit sunflower seeds out the window. I never got tired of it, even when the weather wasn't that great. I got an awful lot of thinking done, puttering along the fields. It was a much simpler way of life. Well, until something broke down, but with my grandfather, fixing things was usually just as entertaining. I wasn't an expert by any means, but it did sound like a nice change of pace. "When's the auction?"

"Tomorrow. If you want, I can put in a good word for you."

Pursing my lips out, I pictured myself standing alone in a field. Not a soul around. The vision was so clear, I could almost smell the fresh cut hay. I could wake up each morning before the sun was up, make coffee, and sip it slowly as I ran the tractor.

Sounds like heaven . . .

After a long quiet moment, Sarg reached the letter forward, placing it on my bare chest. "Well done, Private Mathews. It was a pleasure to serve with you." I was ready for him this time, pulling my left hand to my forehead as he saluted me. Then he turned on his heel and marched out.

I picked up the letter, and flipped it over, examining it. I couldn't even open it with only one hand. This was going to take some getting used to. There were things I would need to relearn. Judging from last night's nightmare, I had a long road ahead. I dropped the letter, letting my gaze float back up to the ceiling where it was most comfortable.

After everything I've been through, it sounds nice to get some land in the middle of nowhere and be alone.

Two

Princess Erralee

A month later

"What do you mean we should surrender!" Father's voice roared through the locked doors of his private study. Pressing my back against the solid wood door, I held my breath, listening.

"I don't care if I must start sending women with babies on their hips to that battlefield! I will not be defeated!" A drawer, or a door of some sort, slammed loudly. "Never say that to me again!" He hollered so terrifyingly loudly it forced me to cringe through my inhalations.

Next came the shrill sound of shattering glass. *More than likely that was his scotch.* I shuddered as I moved my eyes side to side, praying his screaming would stop soon. It had been getting progressively worse all week with phone calls, during meetings with private visitors, back to more phone calls. I was beginning to wonder if it was even safe to stay at the palace, with the war getting so close, but Father refused to evacuate. Cowards leave, as Father put it.

I couldn't take it anymore. My nervous system was beginning to show signs of long-term stress. Never ending nights of insomnia, constant fatigue, and the knot that took up permanent residence in my throat. I could only handle so much. I longed to leave.

I had heard Father's warning about staying inside . . .

I needed a moment alone. Silence. Some fresh air to clear my head. I eased along the wall, careful not to let my heels click on the floor. I hated these shoes with an utter vengeance, but Mother still upheld the stuffy formal royal etiquette rules. *Princesses wear dresses and closed-toed shoes with heels. Don't get me started on the panty hose!* My nostrils flared as Mother's voice echoed in my brain. I was halfway down the hall and finally safe to pick up the pace to run out the back door.

Slipping off my shoes as if they weren't worth the cost of a disposable napkin, I tossed them carelessly in the grass and raced down the path to the forest. My stress melted a little more with each barefoot step. This is where I was most alive. I've explored these woods almost every day of my life. Adoring how the trees echoed with the sound of birdsong, it filled my heart with so much joy and always drew me back to harmony and adventure. Though I believed the true treasures of the forest—the ones that were an ode to its timeless beauty—were found on the unbeaten paths.

I had spent an abnormal amount of time in my youth, hunting for mushrooms. Not because I ate them. I pretended gnomes and fairies hid amongst them. I had every fungus mound memorized with names to accompany them. Storytelling for hours, I would tire, and then sneak into the sun for a refreshing nap. This had been my routine for years, and I couldn't remember it being any other way. Now that I was too old to look for fairies, I still enjoyed an afternoon nap in the sun.

And that is what I positioned myself to do. I made my way to my favorite napping spot, the sunniest place in the field of wild grass. I dropped to the ground, feeling an instant release of anxiety. With each breath I exhaled, my eyelids drifted further down, until finally I was asleep.

"Excuse me, ma'am, but that seat's taken." A deep voice cut through my dreams, startling me from my afternoon slumber.

Sitting up, I arched my chin to get a better look. As my eyes focused, they settled on an imposing man wearing a cowboy hat, a white cotton shirt with rolled-up sleeves, and worn denim jeans, a little too dirty for my taste. But with blue eyes that were more daring than sensitive, he was definitely cute. Okay, the words explosively handsome came to mind, even if he did leave me confused. "There aren't any seats," I declared with assurance.

"Well, yeah that's because it's taken." He raised his tan hand out in a gesture to himself. "You're in *my* field, and it's all taken."

Confused by his lackluster analogy, I dramatically scanned both sides as exasperation seeded in my chest. Nothing but green rolling hills of prairie for miles around. I was certain of that because I'd been napping in this very spot since I was a little girl. Clearly, this man was playing some sort of game. Even if he was handsome, he was being rude. I didn't care for the way he stood way too close, towering over me. His demanding presence made me want to shrink back, or even race out of here. Except for the fact that this was *my* napping spot, I stayed. "But, sir, it's an open field."

Anticipating his lips would curl, and he'd apologize for being rude, I was wrong. He held his gaze steady in a more piercing than inviting manner. "Will you please leave?"

I startled for the second time, and scrambled to my feet, taking care not to trip over my bustling skirt. *Make me!* I yelled in my head, but years of etiquette school had me biting my tongue. *Nobody ever talked to me like that!* Not that I put myself on a pedestal, but people always respected me. Sharply angling my elbow like a spartan cheerleader, I placed one hand on my hip and fumbled for the perfect reply. One to outwit him. One to outsmart him. One to make him feel terrible. "Well, enjoy being lonely!" I sputtered back. "Good day to you, sir!" I spun on my heel and sped off.

I had been enjoying one of the best naps of my life, out in the fresh air, letting the sun warm me with its lullaby rays. Clearly, this rude man wasn't going to let me be. It was better to leave than to argue with stupidity. I tossed a haughty look over my shoulder, and noisily hmphed back before adding in a mutter loud enough for him to hear, "Some people don't know how to treat a lady."

Was it too much to ask for a little politeness? I crossed the field, heading to the worn dirt path leading through the small forest to take me home to the palace. It appeared even the grasshoppers sensed my irritation because they hopped away, keeping their distance as I stormed right through the field. This was undoubtedly the first time I'd ever been interrupted by anyone, let alone told to leave. I was in complete disbelief as I continued to plow my way into the forest.

Even though the forest was thick, if I looked up, I could make out the palace tower's peak standing on the tallest butte. It was a remarkable feat of architecture, with tall pillars draped in ivy, and pearl-white stone walls. Upon my approach to the palace, I made out the intricate carvings that were a nod to my ancestry. Each upper-level room had its own balcony, giving way to breathtaking views of the rolling countryside as far as the eye could see. It was a true fairytale growing up here, and I—a princess—lived in that fairytale.

That was before the war . . .

I found my shoes before I passed through the first set of guards, and I stumbled into them before they could catch me "indecent." I entered the grand courtyard by way of the symmetrical maze of hedges, and statues of seraphim. There was a faster way to enter the palace, around the back, the way the staff entered, but I much preferred to take in its beauty by way of the front entrance. I slowed even more as I passed by the guards who stood tall by the main entrance, not flinching as if they were perfect statues themselves.

My personal guard, Weston, had already made it back and occupied his post. I never quite understood how he managed to do that, because he always lurked in the shadows whenever I was out. As I passed Weston, he slyly reached into his red coat pocket and pulled out a folded paper. Keeping his palm down, he passed it to me as if it were a covert operation.

Without looking at it, I tucked it into my skirt pocket and continued through the main entrance. I stalled, not wanting to run into Father, and meandered through the chamber, taking in each museum-worthy art piece. Something I did daily when I wanted to kill time, but something seemed off. . .

I halted my steps. Several art pieces were missing, including Father's original Monet landscapes. In their place, perfect rectangles outlined the crimson wall paint faded around the spot where the art used to hang. My eyes drifted down the hall, noting many more paintings had vanished. Van Gogh. That didn't disappoint me as much, as none of his art made any sense to me. But the Bouguereau

. . . I paced forward, needing to touch the empty wall for myself. That was my favorite. Where did it go?

What on earth? I scratched my head, and checked back over my shoulder, still in disbelief. If one had needed restoration, the curator would have taken just *one*. Not an entire row.

Rushed footfalls echoed from the corridor, followed by Mother's inquiring voice, "Erralee, honey, where have you been? Your father's been looking for you."

Pivoting slowly on my heel, I pressed a smile on my lips to greet Mother. "Just off in the forest." *Well, until that idiot showed up and ruined it, but you don't need to know about that. Somehow you'd make it my fault.*

"Ah dear, Erralee." Mother's brows bent down thoughtfully, but I couldn't ignore the worry line pinned in the center of her forehead. "I had thought you'd outgrow those nature fantasies by now. It's time you thought about your future."

Mother was never one to argue. She was soft-spoken in nature. The perfect balance to my hot-headed father. If she wasn't happy, she would typically not say anything. It was a little jarring she chose confrontation about this *now*. Sighing, I bit back words of rebuttal and moved closer, reaching an arm out for a side hug. "Ah, mother, I adore nature. There is nothing wrong with that."

"Normally, there isn't." Her thin, red-painted lips pinched as she took a more serious tone. "Your father had a surprise visit from King Aswell. He reigns over an island off the coast of France. His island is filled with mineral mines, and he is *extremely* wealthy. He has dedicated a large amount of his finances to a very impressive military." Mother gave me a dramatic side eye, tacking on, "He is interested in meeting you." She batted her lashes as if to hint that there was something braided in her words. "He wants an heir and is searching for a wife."

I fought like a pack of famished monkeys left with only one banana not to roll my eyes. Instead, I offered a soft shrug. "I don't see how that concerns me."

Mother's lips held tight, not letting another detail about King Aswell slip out. As if to shift the conversation, she pointed to the stairs. "Please hurry and change for dinner."

Letting one foot slide in front of the other, I dragged my feet in obedience. Mother called after me with a tone of urgency, "And do put in the effort to look extra nice." I didn't check over my shoulder. I understood my charging orders. I also didn't doubt Mother would send Margarette, her lady's maid, to assist.

Margarette had done it. I was a vision of beauty, with my raven hair cascading down my back. She had draped my slender figure in the highest luxury silken gown, which shimmered so much it appeared illuminated as I moved through the glow of the muted dinner lights. I didn't feel like smiling, as I hated to be put on display this way. However, as I strode through the grand hall, and caught my father's proud eye, I forced my lips to curve into a gentle smile.

Normally I sat at the end by Mother. Tonight, I was moved to the other side of the table, between Father and King Aswell. On King Aswell's right was my older sister, Ruenella. She also wore her finest dinner dress, and was adorned with so many jewels, she looked more like the queen tonight. I passed her a knowing smile, as I fully understood her out-of-character attire was Mother's idea.

Ruenella was older than me, shy and quiet in public. She was yet to make a lasting impression on any of the men to whom Father had introduced her. Father never hid his disappointment about it either. Maybe Father had lost faith in her ability to date altogether, because this was the first time Father had included me in one of his setups.

Feeling as though my destiny was on the line—and not in a good way—I took my time as I struggled to walk gracefully. My legs grew heavy, each step more and more difficult to maneuver under the weight of this dress.

My throat dried, and I swallowed when I bravely let my gaze meet King Aswell's. His face was stern, bearing a long, hooked nose. He had piercing dark eyes, and deep lines on his face that hardly softened, contrasted by his straw-like, corn-yellow hair. I fought hard to inhale smoothly as the grin he laced on his lips appeared arrogant.

Father stood; his eyes etched with his you-will-be-obedient look, and he motioned to King Aswell as he announced me. "This is my daughter, Princess Erralee."

King Aswell stood stiffly as he raked his eyes over me. "How do you do, Princess Erralee?"

Wouldn't you love to know, you arrogant, skinny, bird-faced geek. I curtsied, lowering my eyes respectfully. "It's a pleasure to meet you."

"Please sit." Father's voice was more commanding than welcoming. I took my spot, sandwiched between both kings. I fought to ignore the tingling in my legs. Every inch of me wanted to hightail it out the door. King Aswell didn't waste a moment to lock his eyes on me. "Erralee, your father tells me you enjoy nature."

For the first time since this man's presence was announced, I felt I'd survive dinner. My shoulders relaxed, and I breathed with slightly more ease. "Yes." Being careful not to talk too much, I coined a concise reply. "I feel peaceful when I'm in the fresh air."

King Aswell gave a slow nod, with his gaze so focused it was more reminiscent of how a doctor examines people, than someone trying to get to know me. "On my island," he went on, "we have rocky terrain that isn't suitable for farming. It has been developed into magnificent stone buildings. Some of the most beautiful churches, libraries, and universities. Being more of an intellectual myself, I don't miss the primitive culture that thrives in rural areas."

"Oh." I tilted away from the king, mulling over whether that had been a cleverly worded insult, or not. Deciding to give the king the benefit of the doubt, I pushed past his comment. "What do you enjoy doing in your free time?"

The king straightened his back even more, as he clearly wore his pride in his posture. "I can spend hours every day reading and researching."

"Reading . . . er," My gaze shifted to the side, as I was never one to sit still long enough to read more than a page at once, especially when inside the palace. Each room had large open balconies which constantly beckoned me to go outside. Nature was always more interesting than words on a page. "That's fascinating. I do enjoy a nice photo book of landscapes," I forced out as I shot a gaze at my sister, who was beaming ear to ear.

Ruenella was brilliant, but had allergies, which made her loathe the outdoors. She was dainty in every way, from her pale skin to her so-blonde-it's-almost white hair. She was a romantic at heart, who dreamed of being courted by a king. It was clear to me she was the better match. I gazed at my sister, thankful the king had more in common with her. I nudged my head toward King Aswell, pleading with my eyes for her to banter with him, but bless her heart for being so shy, she just froze, leaving me to suffer through his small talk.

When dinner was over, Father took King Aswell into the library to take part in his nightly tall glass of scotch and a cigar. It was his only vice, and Mother hated it. Even his doctor warned it was time to cut back, but he was stubborn, persisting. What made it even worse was the way it had now become his social function, and he regularly received gifts of the most expensive cigars, and he vowed it was wasteful not to indulge.

I was ecstatic to be excused to my room, where I immediately changed out of my dinner dress into a linen nightgown, wasting no time retrieving the paper from Weston. In the bustle of getting ushered to dinner I hadn't had time to look at it. My lips curled into a grin steeped in awe. An origami bird, folded from silver cardstock. As I moved his head, his wings flapped, and underneath one of the wings was writing in the tiniest print. A secret.

Caged birds whistle for sovereignty behind golden doors while the feral birds soar.

Erralee, never forget you are the feral bird.

X Weston

My lips curled, holding the secret. Weston was one of the few people who understood my spirit. His single mom had been my nanny when I was younger. We grew up chasing each other around the palace grounds like siblings. He's the one man who saw through my royal façade because he'd grown up behind the curtain. I trusted him with my life. He clearly saw what my parents were up to, trying to pawn me off. This was his way of showing his support.

I shuddered as I recalled King Aswell's face. Father had to be out of his mind to even suggest we'd be a good couple. I reread the writing several times before I resigned myself to staring wistfully out my terrace window. *If only I had real wings . . . Then I could leave this palace forever, and not be subject to Father's rules. Or at least his selfish schemes. He seemed to forget that arranged marriages aren't really a thing in first-world countries. Mother always acted indifferent, as if she thought he was merely joking, but there was nothing funny about the thought of being forced into a marriage that only your father wants.*

I placed the bird in my top vanity drawer, pushing it to the back so the nosey maids wouldn't find it. Then I meandered outside on my private balcony, searching for the owl who had recently built a nest in an older oak tree cavity near the courtyard's edge. He only came out if he didn't see me. Careful to crouch below the terrace spindles, I peered through the vertical slates.

Tonight, he did not disappoint. His eyes glowed gold, his feathers ruffled out, fattening him, while adding to his magnificence. I held my breath, captivated, as he commanded from his nest, so still and wise. Before long, my mind floated to that handsome man I met earlier. Where had he come from? I'd been visiting that spot for years and had never seen him before. His eyes . . . It's like God spent a little more time on those.

They were definitely more alluring than that hooked-nosed king. As annoying as that man was, anything was better than King Arrogant, I mean . . . Aswell.

Three
Reeves

It's funny how getting blasted by a landmine leaves a metallic taste in your mouth. Yanking on my always-stuck kitchen drawer until it flew opened, I easily spotted a pack of breath mints, grabbed it, and popped one in my mouth. Rolling my tongue over it, I tried to dull the metallic sensation. Even after weeks of healing, the taste still lingered. The doctors said it was metal toxicity, and it would go away. I was starting to think that I was going crazy. Strong coffee was the only thing that muted it, but with the main water pipe busted, that meant no coffee at my house.

It'd only been a month since the official discharge from the army, with a prosthetic hand and a pat on the back. It had cost me five years of dedication—and almost my life—now it already felt like a dream.

Except at night.

That was a nightmare.

Nobody warned me about that.

I had hellacious night terrors. I tried switching my diet, and going to bed early but that didn't help. The only thing that stopped them was dropping to my knees, begging for the angels to surround me with their protection. Not the chubby little cherubs you see in gift stores. These days, I go straight to the archangels with swords. The ones I had met on the battlefield. Those are the guys you want on your side.

I chuckled, not because it was funny. It was the kind of thing that if you didn't learn to laugh about it, you'd cry. Crying wasn't going to solve anything. I sought solutions.

That's my motto, and why I was still alive, with civilian freedom. All that was left to do was test out this whole pursuit of happiness thing I had almost died defending.

For me at least, pursuing happiness was a piece of land out in the middle of nowhere.

A fresh start.

Even if it meant repairing this run-down shack from the ground up, I'd get it done. This little house had been vacant for years. A decade ago, it had housed a family who worked for the king on his farms. It wasn't much compared to the huge plots of land the modern industrial farms managed. It also wasn't enough land to make a living on. I was working on acquiring more land. For right now, this was home.

With the busted pipe in my hand, I slipped on my boots, and headed out the side door, doubting this small-town hardware store had the pipe I needed. I took long strides, rounding the side of the house, and instantly spotted something off in the distance.

Or rather some*one.*

She wasn't trying to hide her whereabouts either be-cause she was wearing a banana-yellow dress that could have been seen from Mars. *That woman is sleeping in my field again!*

It's not that I had anything against neighbors, or naps. I rather loved naps and sometimes felt neighborly. However, I came here to isolate myself. I didn't want this woman—or anybody for that matter—becoming *too* neighborly. I had a fence for a reason. *This isn't public picnic land!*

"Hey lady," I called out, pacing toward her. I didn't want to frighten her, but I needed to warn her sternly. "I told you this is private land."

She had something in her where she didn't cower. She scampered to her feet and stared at me. Now that I was close, I could see her eyes were colored like the midnight sky. They had just enough spark in them, that I didn't feel sorry for her.

"Didn't you notice I was sleeping!" she hollered with audacity as if I was the one in the wrong. Her fists balled at her sides, and she retorted, "I was literally having the best dream, and you wrecked it with your big-bear voice."

I'd been called many names before, but never had any-one insulted my voice. Before I checked my attitude, I called back, "Big Bird called. He wants his drip back."

"Pardon me?" Her hand perched on her hip, and her mouth opened and closed a couple of times before finally saying, "Are you seriously calling me fat?"

"No!" I spurted back, as she was so delusional, she didn't get the comparison. "I was calling you *yellow*."

"Oh." She regarded her dress and sealed her lips. Her *barefoot* feet still didn't budge. A sense of entitlement showed through her elevated posture when she stared back at me. "I'm going to have to ask you to run along, so I can get back to my nap."

"Me run along?" I jerked my thumb toward my chest. "*You* need to run along." I wiggled two fingers like legs in front of her face as if they were running. "This is my land, and if I have to call the sheriff and report you for trespassing, I will."

"Your land?" She checked behind her shoulders as if she expected someone to support her. "Do you know who my father is?"

"I don't care if your father is the king, because even he doesn't own this land." I bit my lip, doing my best to tame the grin I was brewing as I destroyed her lofty superiority.

"Wait." She held a hand to her temple and blinked several times. "What did you say?"

"I said—" I made a sweeping gesture out toward the field, but she cut me off.

"—No, I heard what you said, but you're wrong. My father *is* the king, and this is *his* land." She stared at me as if she had laid the trump card.

I would imagine if my father were king, I'd have gotten used to throwing his name around, but not this time. I had almost died defending this country for the tyrant king, and used the measly little active duty pay I'd received to buy this scrap of land. I *earned* it. "Correction." I held up an imposing finger. "It *was* his land. He sold it to me last week."

Her head sprang back, and a bewildered look flashed on her face. Apparently, her dear old dad didn't tell her what he was up to. Daddy's little princess was about to learn some hard truths. "Now, what were you saying?" Leaning toward her, I tacked on, "Why don't you run along and ask your daddy whose land this is."

Her brows angled down sharply while her lips parted, but no words fell out. Instead, she spun on her heel, running toward the forest.

She was gone. Satisfied, I brushed my hands together and turned back to my Dodge Ram.

Problem solved.

Four
Princess Erralee

Several times today I pushed that rude cowboy out of my mind, but as much as I tried, his cocky smile kept popping back into my head, taunting me. I was about at my wit's end, trying to ignore him, when I decided to confront Father about the land. I paced forward into my father's study, finding him alone, resting with his eyes closed in a high-back armchair in front of his fireplace. A taller than normal glass of dark scotch sat on the end table next to him. It was a bit jarring to see him drinking that much, especially since he was alone.

Not wanting to disturb him, I took one step back out, but he opened his eyes. The shadows under them were grayer than the last time I saw him. Even though I felt bad for the stress he was under, it didn't stop my curiosity. "Father, who is that man living in the old Barnes house?"

"Last name's Mathews," his voice was vague, and dull, as if he was recalling the most boring part of life. He seemed to be disassociating a little more every day that the war went on. "Just got back from war. Lost an arm."

I took another step toward him, hoping to catch some facial expressions, since I couldn't tell from his words if he was speaking the whole truth. "Did you . . . sell that land to him?"

He retrieved his glass of scotch, running his thumb methodically along the rim. Around and around, I watched him rub his glass. "I did."

"Why would you do that?" My eyes narrowed, taking this loss personally. Father understood that was my favorite place on earth. I loved it more than this castle, and that was hard to do because I loved my home immensely.

"Someday you will understand." His words seemed so disjointed. Not at all as if they were even meant to be strung together. This conversation gave me the sense that my father was lost. He was acting completely out of character, and not at all like his normal direct and boastful self. "You might as well know now that I've formed an alliance with King Aswell."

"Ohhh." My voice dropped into a whisper. Something in the air was off. Father's voice was abnormally calm and stable. Not at all like his dramatic persona that enhances when he drinks.

"He's agreed to use his military to protect us. He speaks as if he's sure he can put an end to this war, but he's asked for your hand in marriage, and I've agreed."

"W-what?" I stuttered out. Father's words went completely over my head. Clearly something had gone horribly wrong with my hearing. Nothing about what he said made sense. "Excuse me, but what did you say?" I turned my head, leaning my ear in.

"I said, you're getting married to King Aswell." He raised his plump index finger, wagging it at me, reminiscent of a child who needed scolding. "The decision is made."

I blinked, taking his words like a bullet into my gut. The stern expression he fixed on me wasn't one to argue with. I'd tried that before and always failed. Yet, I couldn't stand here and remain quiet. I couldn't stand here at all . . . I spun on my heels and fled from his study.

No doubt about it, the most gut-punching thing that could happen in life is having the man who God appointed to protect you, end up being the man who was solely responsible for destroying your future.

Or maybe that's just the busting of the biggest lie I'd ever been told. Maybe Father's goal never was to protect me? Maybe it was always about preserving his name and fortune.

I scurried up the front staircase, not sure where I was going until the rumble in my stomach got too hard to ignore, and I burst through the bathroom door. The bitterness of bile diluted the burn of stomach acid as the two fluids meshed, searing my esophagus. The heat of vomit flooded my mouth before cresting my throat. Parting my lips over the porcelain toilet, I let it spill, and cried out, "I would rather die than marry that man!"

I shuddered, recalling my father's announcement. I was blindsided. He didn't even ask my opinion. It was as casual as telling me we were having soup for dinner. No emotion.

Swiping my mouth with the sleeve of my gown, I pulled myself off the marble floor and sniffed back tears. I fled to my room. Ruenella found me in the hallway, falling into step with me. She beckoned, "Erralee, you don't have a choice."

"So, you knew about this too?" I barked out, disgustedly.

She ignored my ill tone. "The front-line army is depleted, and all the other countries are abandoning us, and pulling their troops. They are opening the draft. Our people are dying. King Aswell promised his military in exchange for your hand in marriage. His army is the strongest and most feared. They could end this overnight. Everything will return to normal if you do this for our country."

"Our people?" I glared at her, a growing wedge of disagreement swelled between us.

No, our friends. And if you think he's so wonderful, why don't you offer to marry him?

Nobody wanted this war to end more than I did. This war was defining half of my generation, because it killed the other half.

Still, two wrongs—or even thousands of wrongs—can never magically become a right . . . no matter how hard I wished it would be enough.

I fought the defeated sigh, that begged for release, by burying every thought of surrender deep into my gut. I didn't need a reminder of any of the war injustices. I was haunted by Father's hollowed-out, jumbled words as they rang over and over in my head.

My own Father had *sold me*!

I'd rather *die* than be used as a pawn in twisted war games. Even if it meant my country would be forced to continue an unjust war. Father was wrong. My country would be better off winning this war through its own blood and sweat.

I would be better off . . . disappearing.

"The only way that man will ever have my hand is if he chops it off." I spit out with disgust. I shivered as I blew through the open bedroom door, and headed to my walk-in closet, studying the garments in front of me. Everything hung neatly on perfect white hangers. Dresses made from the finest silks, bedazzled with jewels, and matching cashmere wraps. Raised as any modern princess would be, I had never wanted for anything materially, and it showed in my closet.

With seconds ticking away on the clock, I understood all too well that the only way I could get out of this marriage was if I kept time on my side.

I would pack nothing.

"Who am I kidding? I won't need any of this anymore," I murmured as I closed the doors and hurried across the room, back out into the hall, not stopping until I got to the back staircase, which was reserved for staff. I barreled down the steps, ready to slip out the back door.

I halted on my heel swiftly as ice ran through my veins.

King Aswell was in the middle of the hall, blocking my passage with a large velvet box in his hand. Slowing my steps, I straightened my spine and proceeded cautiously with a polite curtsy. "King Aswell."

"I suppose you think you are going to run away." His voice was smooth, but not condescending. He tipped his head toward me in a way that appeared humble, especially when I compared his stance to the way my father stood, tall, and stiff. His eyes were black as coal, and even though he didn't do anything to make his expression harsh, the darkness of his eyes gave me shivers.

How did he even know to wait for me here? This staircase was for staff. I tossed a look back over my shoulder, and all the way down both ends of the empty hallway. No one was around. It made no sense for King Aswell to take a post here, unless my parents had this entire castle secured. My chin quivered through my denial. "I was going to the forest."

"I won't stop you." He didn't waver from his stance blocking me, letting the pause in the conversation drag on for several beats. "Let it be known that if you do run, your father will banish you forever. Your kingdom will lose everything." His gaze lowered to the velvet box, and he studied it as if seeing it for the first time, before pushing it forward. It wasn't a gentle push, or even something that was hurried from the normal excitement you have when you present someone with a gift. It was an oddly smooth whisking motion, reminding me of how a snake slithers. Quiet. Calculated.

"What's that?" I eyed it suspiciously while heat scorched my cheeks.

"It's a small symbol of the life I'm offering you." He continued to present the box, but there was no way I was going to take it. "There's a festival tonight in the town square, and I'd like to announce our engagement. Please know if you become my wife, you will be my greatest treasure."

I turned my cheek away from the box as if it stung to look at it. "With all-due respect," I squeaked out, "there's been some mistake. We don't even know each other."

I studied his pattern of speech patiently, as I waited through his pause before he said, "Getting to know each other is not how aristocratic families make bonds."

I tried to resist a sour expression as he spoke so business-like about the engagement. Even the way he stood a proper two feet away, with perfect posture, as if we were negotiating a business contract, made my stomach ill. *This wasn't the life I had wanted. Did I get a say?*

He filled the silence with a low, even tone, "Your father is at the end of his resources. He's sold most of his royal farm-land, art, jewels, and the national debt cannot be raised any more, but *you* can help him . . ." He slowly opened the box; the hinges creaked a little, evidence that the box was old, and whatever was inside was an heirloom. A gold choker, with so many blue diamonds it was impossible to count them in one sweep of the eye, sparkled at me.

Swallowing, I rubbed my neck and sucked in a quiet gasp of air as I stared into the center diamond. The light reflected off the diamond, drawing me into a light trance. The metaphorical metal cinching tighter and tighter, the room appeared to spin, and all I saw was my unhappy future with this horrid man. My airway got tighter until I finally broke my gaze from the diamond, and I was left panting. The irony of his gift being a jeweled choker was the perfect symbol of what this arrangement was to be. Stunning in all the measurements of the world, but it was merely a chain. I didn't want any part of it.

Without blinking I held his gaze. "Why me? Why not my sister? You two have much more in common."

Instead of replying, he removed the choker from the box, and painfully slowly brought it to my neck. He paused, holding the choker inches from me. His body heat permeated off his hands, making me cringe. "May I?"

"I don't know why you bothered to ask. You didn't even ask my permission to marry me." It wasn't a polite response, but it was my most honest thought. My mind was at a crossroads. One, I couldn't see far on either path. If I didn't marry this man, this war would rage forever . . . and so many people had already died, and our country would be in ruins. The stress of it all was sure to kill my father because his health had already suffered so much. Then my mother would be left to care for this broken kingdom, and I wouldn't want that either.

"You are beautiful." King Ashwell's measured words broke my thoughts as he draped the necklace around my neck. I stiffened at his touch, but he continued. "Your eyes have a fire I've not seen before." His hands were warm against my flesh as he connected the choker's clasp. I sucked in a sharp breath when I felt the cinch. "It's your spirit," he almost whispered, his hands still on my throat even though the necklace was fastened. He finally lowered his hands to his side and stepped back. His gaze penetrated me, giving me the biggest wave of the creeps. "I'm offering you anything you want, and your country will be saved."

My chin quivered, as if an earthquake lived inside my jaw. This was an impossible choice.

Of course, I wanted the war to end.

Of course, I wanted my father to have this huge burden lifted from him.

However, I didn't want to marry a stranger. I felt nothing but disgust for this old man. He was practically Father's age.

As if he sensed my trepidation, he lowered his voice. "I'm not going to force this. It's up to you, but I also won't wait forever." He reached forward, beckoning for my hand, and I timidly placed it in his. He was gentle as he brought my hand to his lips and pressed a kiss to the top of my fingers. Without another word, he let go and left.

My hand trembled. Unsure of what that meant, I doubted it was the start of any affection. Maybe I could eventually get there, but right now, I was repulsed.

I peered down the hall, not seeing any staff, but the knot in my gut twisted, and even though I couldn't see anyone, I was being watched. It obviously wasn't safe to flee now. I'd have to be more discreet. That meant I would have to convince them I would stay until they let their guard down. For now . . . I'd have to play along. I'd have to go to the festival tonight and let them all think I would do precisely what they wanted.

Five

Reeves

A piece of land was my first ingredient to a fresh start. The second was my Dodge Ram I named Dusty. He wasn't new; not even close, but new-enough-to me.

The third ingredient to a fresh start was driving Dusty dangerously fast. The smell of burning rubber dulled the taste of iron, while pumping me full of adrenaline shots to counter the constant surge of cortisol I'd been living with for years.

I cranked the wheel, pulling over to the corner of Main Street. I barely found a parking spot, as the downtown streets were blocked off. They were setting up an event of some sort. When I hopped out of my truck, I inhaled crisp, clean air that was a bit chillier than usual for this time of year. An early snowstorm had been in the forecast for later this week. That meant I needed to hustle to fix my broken pipe. My worn boots left a faint dust I'd picked up from my scoria crusted driveway as I walked to the diner, and I rattled the old-fashioned bell jingle as I opened the door.

New to town, you'd think the tight-knit locals wouldn't have much to say, but it turned out I was the fresh gossip they craved, especially the old blue-haired ladies who played pinochle here in the mornings. This was my third time stopping here this week, and I noticed a pattern. The chatter in the diner immediately quieted as soon as I walked through the door.

I was unbelievably good at getting people to shut up.

That part wasn't so bad.

I could feel their eyes on me, and today the counter lady called out, "New guy, how's it going?"

"Can't feel my hand." It was a joke, but the counter lady didn't know my sense of humor and sealed her lips shut from further inquiries. The squint in her gaze as it slid briefly to my prosthetic told me how she really felt. *Uncomfortable.* I stuck that hand in my pocket and rushed to change the subject. "I'll have a black coffee."

She pushed up the bill of her uniform hat, letting her hair net peek out. She was everyone's scary lunch lady from grade school. All she was missing was a wart on her nose, and a giant spoonful of brussels sprouts. "I'm making a fresh pot. If you can wait one minute, it'll be ready."

I gave a curt nod and pulled out a counter stool.

"How's fixing up the old Barnes farmstead?" the counter lady asked as she readied a large Styrofoam cup and lid.

"It's fine." I ran my tongue along my teeth, pushing the mint around, already not impressed with this conversation.

"They always did have issues with their water." Her head dipped in a confirming bob. "Had to haul the drinking stuff from town."

I pressed my lips together. The only thing I hated more than small talk was *nosey* small talk.

"Course," the counter lady went on, "that's what you get for not building a basement in this part of the country. You're just asking for frozen—" The pot gurgled a tad forcefully, drawing her attention back to it. "Oh, it's done." She grabbed the pot and poured the piping hot coffee into the cup. While she was adding the lid, she tacked on, "You know, if you need any help in the fields, Tilly Wagner has a whole slew of young boys who are strong. She's always needing some extra money, with her husband running off and all—"

"Thank you." I took the cup out of her hand and tossed a ten-dollar bill on the counter. I didn't have the stomach for gossip. Never was one for small talk. I'd also learned the hard way that those that gossip with you, will surely end up gossiping about you.

"Did you see them setting up for the Fall Festival? It should be starting any moment." The counter lady quickly switched conversations as she grabbed my money and punched numbers into the cash register. Without telling me a total, she dropped change into my hand. "The king hosts a festival every year in the town square, and everyone is invited."

Grimacing, I tried not to complain, but I already knew about the festival. When I closed on my plot of land, King

D'Long personally welcomed me to town and invited me to join them. Normally, I'd never go to anything like that. I hated crowds. My anxiety couldn't handle them.

The catch was . . . I still had my eye on two more plots of the king's land. He said they weren't for sale. I hoped to make a good impression and get him to change his mind. Which meant, if the king asked me to come to his festival—and he had—I had to at least make an appearance.

Maybe I'd get lucky and get a chance to talk to him about the land? If not, I could always duck out early. I shoved my change into my pocket, tipped my hat toward the lady, and left.

With coffee in hand, I stepped back out on the sidewalk and headed down the street to the hardware store. Just as I thought, they didn't have what I needed, but I got it ordered. With no water back home, I figured I might as well stick around for dinner at the festival.

Street musicians played loud country music. I wasn't much for crowds, but I didn't mind a good band. As I wandered toward the beat, I passed several food trucks, which smelled so mouth-wateringly delicious that my stomach growled. I wasn't a foodie, but it'd been a while since I'd had savory food like that. Lured by a BBQ food truck with a fat cartoon pig on the outside, I got in line.

If I had felt out of place in this small town all week, now I felt like a giant with four heads. Everyone was paired off in private circles, talking as if they'd all known each other their entire lives. As I stood in line, I'd randomly catch someone staring at me—or rather my hand—before they slid their gaze away.

I sighed, not feeling the least bit offended.

When I got to the front of the line, they had crossed out most of the menu items as being sold out already. The only thing left was pulled pork sandwiches or baby-back ribs. They both sounded good, but if I wanted to eat ribs, I had to sit down. The tables were crowded, and I did NOT want to sit by anyone. "I'll have a sandwich."

Thankfully, the two guys who were working didn't ask any personal questions as they handed over the basket and pointed to the napkin dispenser. I grabbed one and stepped out of the line. As I surveyed the growing crowd, I eased along the back while listening to the music.

The band played from a small stage set up in the middle of the road, and they weren't too shabby. They looked to be about my age, perhaps even in college. Meandering around the tables and away from the crowd, I spotted a little tent with royal guards.

I came here to see the king, and so that's obviously where I need to be . . .

I nonchalantly placed one foot in front of the other, pretending not to notice the area was roped off. This was going to be so easy— A mammoth guard stepped out in front of me from nowhere, and I smacked into him. "Hi," I blubbered as I bounced back and arched my chin to see his face. The dude was a giraffe.

"This area's roped off." His lips didn't crack a smile, and the intense glare he planted on me warned me not to push him. The last thing I needed was an altercation in my first week in town. That wasn't how I was going to impress the king.

"Oh." I made a large O shape with my lips, pretending only now to notice the guarded area. "I was looking for the bathrooms. I thought it was in this tent."

"Bathrooms are by the food trucks."

"Great. I'll head over . . . that way," I pointed to indicate I was leaving as I turned on my heel. So much for that plan. I stuffed the last of my sandwich into my mouth and decided to call it a night. I didn't know what I'd been thinking. I wasn't going to get near the king tonight. Now that my belly was full, home sounded great.

The entrance area was packed with people. Just the sight of them all lined up, waiting to get in made my stomach knot. I didn't want to weave through them while they all stared at me as if I was the newest museum exhibit. My gaze skirted toward the back alley. That was clear. I could jump the fence and go that way. Yeah, it's a detour, but that's where I was with this whole people thing. I would rather walk miles to avoid one person. People meant questions, and I was done answering questions.

The people annoyed me, but this band was fantastic. I focused on the lyrics, and it sure helped to keep my anxiety attacks at bay. I missed live music. So much so, I was almost whistling by the time I ducked into the alley. As I rounded the corner, my eyes caught sight of someone.

A woman so radiantly dressed in a gown fit for a fairytale wedding she seemed to glow from her position against the brick building. What made me stop wasn't her appearance. Rather, the sobs of distress. She was bawling as if she was in extreme agony. As much as I avoided people, I couldn't let a person suffer. "Ma'am," I infused my voice with empathy. "Is there something I can help you with?"

Continuing to weep into her hands, she didn't lift her face, and I pulled toward her. *Maybe she needs a doctor?* "What's wrong? Can I call for help?" I offered, taking further steps closer.

"Nobody can help me." Her words fell between broken sobs. "It's just fate."

"Whoa, whoa, whoa," I cautioned. "Nothing is ever out of your hands. Someone can do something. What's wrong?" I pressed again. My military instincts had taken over. I sensed she was in trouble. "If you're in danger," I whispered in case she was being spied on, "tap your foot."

"I'm not in danger," she exclaimed, dropping her hands to reveal her face. "Unless you think being forced to marry a man you don't even know is unsafe?"

When her fiery eyes met mine, a shiver ran right through me. She looked awfully familiar. I tapped my chin, wondering where I'd seen her before.

Before I had a chance to place her, she called it. "You again!"

"Me?" I immediately got defensive, taking a step back.

Her face had already been a shade of red from all the crying she had been doing, but somehow it managed to flush even deeper, into a shade of crimson, as she pointed an accusing finger in my face. "You're that man from the field."

My brain slammed back to earlier. Before I could check my manners, and well, I didn't really want to have manners because she bothered me, I yelled, "You're that annoying, spoiled princess who keeps trespassing on my land!"

She squared her body with mine but didn't utter a sound as she stood slack jawed, ogling me as if nobody had ever said anything true to her before.

Rolling my hand over my forehead, my annoyance budded. *This is why I don't talk to people. I know better than to stop. Even if I am only trying to help, I always end up with the most annoying people. I could be in my truck by now. Now, I'm stuck trying to talk my way out of this.*

"Sorry to bother you." I slid one foot in front of the other, hoping to make a clean break from this encounter. "Now that I know you're not in danger, I'll leave you alone." I didn't look back as I took steps back out the alley. *I'd gladly walk back through that crowd ten times rather than talk to* her! What is she even doing here? Shouldn't she be in her high-security-snob tent?

"You don't have to run off," she annoyingly called after me. "I could use someone to talk to."

"Ah," I tried to speak over my shoulder, but her shaky-teared voice made me look back. "I'm not good at talking." She pressed her hands to her face, wiping new tears. As hard as my heart had become, I could never walk away from a woman crying. My insides froze.

"I can't talk to anyone in my family about this." She was sobbing again. "They are all counting on me to marry King Aswell, so he commits to ending this war." She threw her hands out in question. "I don't even know him, let alone want to get married. If I don't do it," she rambled, her voice growing urgent and more afraid, "this war will continue *forever*. My father will have to sell everything. The rest of the art, our farmland, and—"

Ping!

My brain shuddered through the words. *Her dad, the king, will SELL the rest of his land . . .* And I pivoted, turning back to her, my eyes laser-focused on her lips. "What did you say?"

She swiped her nose and sniffed through a few hiccup sobs. I read her lips as she spoke. "The king who wants to marry me has a powerful military. He promised to end this war *if* I marry him." Her lips pinched in agony and another weep tumbled out. "But I can't marry a man I don't know!"

"You can't," I echoed, my brain connecting the dots of her rambled story. Apparently, her dad would sell the land *unless* she got married. If she gets married . . . he wouldn't need to sell the land. My eyes grew large, and I was seeing this whole situation of mine—and hers—in a new light.

She can't get married!

That will be terrible for me! I'll never get my land, and I won't be able to farm enough to live off the land I have. I'll have to move back to some overpopulated city, get a city job and drown in all the people! "Oh, no," I breathed out with so much concern I almost got dizzy. "You can't get married. That's a terrible idea."

"What?" Her voice quivered from the lingering sobs, but she shot me a quizzical look. "You don't think I should do it to save our kingdom? People are dying."

"I don't . . ." I shook my head, feeling how wrong this whole situation was for me. I was so close to getting more land. I could have cattle, and hay, and earn enough to live and never have to go anywhere near anybody. If she got married, and the war ended, the country would grow strong. I wanted that. Of course, I wanted this country to flourish, but *not before I got my land*! To get information, I asked questions in a casual tone, "So, your dad is pretty stressed?"

"Yes." Her voice was somber. "There's been a lot of developments with . . . things."

"Interesting," I mused while I rubbed my chin. "Does he sound desperate?" I winced, and quickly tacked on, "I mean, it has to be so stressful to be a powerful king in charge of so many people's lives."

"He must be desperate to do this." Her eyes pinched, teasing more tears. I honestly don't know where she was getting them from at this point. She had to be about dehydrated.

"Good," I accidentally blurted out, and rushed to cover, "I mean, good that's, he's, um, er." I bit my tongue as this wasn't working. "Does he need help? Can I offer help?" I stammered with a new approach. "I could *buy* something . . ."

"He needs a lot of help. Which is why I must do this . .
." Her voice trailed off, and underneath the lingering tears,
there was a solid conviction that scared me.

"You can't marry a man you don't love," I blurted. I was
begging, ready to take a knee in front of her. This was both
of our last chances at happiness. "It's a . . . betrayal of your
own self." I was never what you call a romantic type, as I
was practical about everything. I honestly didn't care if she
wanted to marry a monkey, but at this point, I was invested
in this marriage. I need some sort of fantasy to sell her to
put off this marriage until *after* I have my land.

"Think about everything you'd miss out on," I urged.
She hiked a curious brow, which confirmed I was taking
this argument in the right direction. "Love is life's greatest
treasure. You can't give up on that, before you even try."
My gaze bored into her eyes, pleading. "You're a beautiful
woman, who probably has an amazing personality. *Wait.*"
I squeezed my hands into fists, pleading. "*Wait* to marry
until you find that special person who sees *you*, and not
just your royal position."

Her lashes fluttered, blinking back more tears, but her
voice was slightly stronger. "I never thought of it that way."

"Think about it this way," I echoed, nodding repeatedly
like a bobble head. "You deserve to *wait* to marry someone
you love more than anything. Someone who makes your
heart flutter just being near them. Someone who would *die*
for you, finishes your sentences, and loves you for—"

"F-for me," she rushed to complete my sentence. Before
I even understood what was happening, we both fell silent.

Our gazes entwined as if we were both given the privilege to peek behind a hidden layer in the other. It's that moment you see in fairy tales, boy meets girl or whatever you called it. Even though we weren't meeting for the first time, something felt off—or instead *on* about the moment. Call it a redo or take two. A spark or an explosion. I didn't care what you named it. *Something* happened, and I was too scared to move.

Her eyes widened, revealing all the glistening specks of her emotions like blue-violet ripples pulsating around her pupils.

"Yeah," I whispered, feeling the reverie linger, only to seep deeper into my chest. "For you," I echoed. Then quickly tacked on with a tilt of my head, "Who *are* you?"

"Erralee," Her voice was slightly more potent than mine, making me doubt she was experiencing the same thing I was. *What was happening?*

"Reeves." I didn't force a smile, and I couldn't pull my gaze from her. I feared she'd disappear the moment I looked away, because even though she looked completely real, there was still something so surreal I proceeded with extreme caution.

Like in the movies, the band in the background suddenly crescendos, pulling our attention to the up-tempo swing beat. I was clearly out of my mind as I reached my hand forward, making my intentions clear that I was requesting a dance. *I was in a trance. What do they call these things? Love spells. Whatever it was, I had it. All I wanted to do was be near her. Which is absurd because I hate people.*

Wait, this wasn't a real attraction. It can't be. I'm clearly just desperate to get her to stop her wedding. Yeah . . . that's why I'm acting this way. I need her to like me, so she doesn't like her fiancé.

Her lashes lowered, but her sweet smile curled on her lips. "I don't know these steps."

"It's just the jitterbug," I pressed my hand out further, insisting. "I'll teach you." Her head turned away, declining. I was out of my mind and stepped forward, slipping my arm around her. I'd never been so forward with a woman, or felt so thoroughly in my place as I did right now. My mind was going full throttle through all the things. *Did she really smell this amazing, like fields of lilies and honey, or am I just disoriented by my desperation to stop this wedding?*

She allowed me to guide her forward, and I eased her into the steps, back and then under my arms. When she came out giggling, I knew I could speed it up, and I did.

Jitterbugging, for me, was a high-intensity sport. The more twists I could add to it, the better, and it didn't take me long to see Erralee was a willing dance partner. Nobody would even be able to tell I was missing a real hand. Truthfully, this was one of the first times I didn't notice I was missing a hand. I wasn't as focused on my body as I was her smile. Her lips curled across her whole face, enough to make dimples ripple on each cheek. Each time I flung her under my arms, she let out an airy giggle like she was on the most fun roller coaster ride, which only encouraged my big ego to dance faster.

I was on a mission to make her like me, and the more she giggled, the more I accepted that as a green light. She kept up, only missing steps a few times, but we quickly picked back up, carrying on until the song was over. We twirled until we couldn't hold on for another moment, breaking our hold of each other, and we were left standing a proper arm's length apart.

My lips parted, about to speak, when royal trumpets blared. Erralee's brows instantly shot to the sky. "I must go! They're announcing my father. He'll be livid if I'm not there."

"Wait—" I reached forward, fingers grasping at the air, but she was gone. I knew not to follow her. Something had happened that I couldn't explain. A stirring in my heart I hadn't ever felt, but I had to be crazy for feeling this way.

Erralee is a princess who is engaged to a king. She is beautiful, and I let her beauty distract me for a second.

This was clearly just my anxiety. I'm so stressed out about finding a way to pay my bills. A blip in my heart, only confusing me. Shaking my head, releasing the last of my fantasy, I turned and walked back to Dusty.

Now, back to fixing that pipe.

Six

Princess Erralee

Desperate to return to the tent, before Father noticed I was gone, I scurried toward the trumpets. The sun was blazing at that awkward evening angle where you can't see anything, and I ran smack into Weston as soon as I hit the street. If I hadn't immediately recognized him by the locks of blond hair sticking out the side of his hat, I would have screamed in fright.

He always had that past-due haircut look. It wasn't proper for any military, but since he often went undercover in public, nobody made him cut it. Well, and because I preferred him this way. It's how I always knew him, my childhood friend with a bit of an edge. He pushed every boundary, but not enough that he would get in trouble. It was his art, and he wasn't afraid of anything. That's why I felt so safe with him.

He waved me forward. "I'm happy to cover for you, but let me know where you're going." His tone was disapproving, but his mischievous grin said how he really felt. He was glad I was safe, and amused that I got away from him *again*.

"One of these days you're going to get me fired if anyone notices I'm not with you."

"Sorry about that." I winced through nervous eyes. It hadn't dawned on me how long I was gone. I let out a deep breath, inducing my forced calm as I fell into stride with him en route to the tent. As much as Weston's presence calmed me, the task before me had my heart ripped open.

Dread settled within me. Father had been loving toward me my entire life. Sure, I wanted to make him proud, but this was a betrayal. He was fulfilling it in the most gruesome way. A public performance to lock me into this lie. He understood if I backed out after tonight, the entire country would blame me for the continuation of the war. I'd never be able to show my face again. There was no use talking to Father either, but . . .

Perhaps I can talk to King Aswell?

Before I found my father, I scoured the tent for King Aswell. I let out a sigh of relief when I saw him standing alone, away from Father. He was impeccably dressed in a long black velvet coat which nearly clung to the ground. It had rich gold piping all along the bottom edges, and I didn't doubt the gold was real. Though his skin was olive toned and his eyes only held dark hues, black really wasn't his best color. It set off an ominous vibe, and just like that, a giant shadow, the size of a tree, broad, powerful, and potent, encased my heart.

As if he was reading my mind, King Aswell's gaze fell on me, and he started pacing toward me. I held my breath. *Please be more understanding than Father.* A mere moment later, he was by my side with a furrowed brow. He dispensed with traditional greetings. "You are hesitant." His expression was not unkind, but it still didn't feel familiar.

Pushing my fingers into my temples, I paused to find the right words without offending him. "It's a lot of pressure," I finally managed while still afraid to look at him. "I would feel better if we could slow down, and go a more traditional route, getting to know each other before we made everything so public."

His breath was heavy, crackling in the air between us, aiding the feeling that the world was closing in on me. "That's understandable."

"What?" Used to my father's totalitarian ruling style, I wasn't expecting a sympathetic response. My heart hammered in my chest as I searched his face for help.

"I don't wish you to live your life afraid of me." His look of concern morphed into an appreciative grin. "I would love the chance to get to know you."

"Then why are we rushing—" I dropped my question because I had the answer. "My father wants to rush, right?"

"He's eager to end this war. I can't commit my country's resources until we have a proper union. It's not fair to my country because this isn't our enemy." He lowered his gaze thoughtfully, parting his lips as if his words were waiting to come out. *He is going to apply some ultimatum.* When he finally did speak, he surprised me. "If you choose to marry me, my country would be very blessed to have you as their queen."

His words were sincere. As hard as I tried to want this—because it would solve everything—I had nothing but a feeling of doom pounding in my chest.

"Perhaps," he interrupted my thoughts, "I can talk to your father. I will suggest we wait a week. There's no reason why this announcement needs to be tonight. I'll delay my return home, and we can spend the week together if that would make you more comfortable."

I should have let out a breath of relief, but I didn't feel relieved. If anything, the chokehold that had been placed on me tightened up another notch. If my option was now or delaying this a week, neither choice was promising. After seven more days, I'd be right back to this moment again, trying to force myself into something I didn't want to do.

Unless spending time with him will help me to see him differently? It would be nice to end this war. Maybe I will feel better in a week? It would be worth trying.

"If that's an option you're okay with, I'd agree to wait another week." My voice was firm, reinforcing my decision to at least try to like him.

My gaze fled to my father's back. Before I could say anything more, King Aswell spoke again, "I'll tell him it was my idea." He offered a reassuring smile and left to join my father.

I couldn't sleep that night. Even though, I was panicked about King Aswell, my mind wandered to Reeves. I actually found myself smirking as I recalled the carefree way he had flung me around. It was a simple moment. It was something I had been missing out on. I'd never danced in a public place, or even been alone with a man. We weren't trying to put on a show for an audience or look royal as I'm forced to do at our palace balls. It was a slice of regular life. Something I hadn't ever experienced. I didn't have a plastic smile glued on my face to give the appearance I was having fun, but I genuinely enjoyed myself and laughed for real.

I had never been allowed to mingle with whomever I wanted. Weston was always standing way too close for anyone to approach me. If I hadn't snuck out when he was looking the other way, he wouldn't have allowed it.

How would it be if I could go about my day without always having to be a princess? Tears budding in the back of my eyes, leaving me curious. *Would I be* happy? Do I even know what happiness is?

I understood my privilege. I wasn't complaining as I had opportunities most people only dreamed about. Still, I enjoyed remembering that stolen dance on the street. It might be the most fun I'd had.

Ever.

That was really sad.

My lips turned down as I realized my entire life was actually depressing. I was like the caged bird Weston wrote about, and Father was my ruler.

The night skies morphed into early dawn, and sleep evaded me. By morning, I laid in bed, groggy and forlorn. Growing more bitter with each passing hour.

"Erralee," Ruenella's voice sang from the other side of my bedroom door.

"Come in." I sat up, eyes barely landing on my door before it opened faster than I had anticipated for a lazy Saturday. Ruenella bounded in, her brightly painted lips beaming ear to ear. Her blonde curls piled on top of her head and cascaded down like never-ending silk waves. There wasn't a day she wasn't fully made up. She was always stunning, in contrast to me, who preferred to dress more plainly. Before I could greet her, she blurted out, "King Aswell is downstairs! Father is requesting that you come down at once."

"What?" I ran my hand over my hair, attempting to smooth it down. I had gone to bed with it still wet, because I liked how it left soft waves in my hair. Mother always preferred it to have texture, and if it wasn't wavey, she'd force Margarette on me with her curling iron and sprays.

Since I didn't sleep, but rather tossed all night, my plan to have soft curls backfired, leaving my hair ratted. It wasn't anywhere near Mother's standards. I flipped my blanket off me and darted to my closet, nervously scanning my dresses. Both my parents would insist I present with my best, but I wasn't ready for this! *Isn't he supposed to call first?*

I fanned through my day dresses, tossing most aside. Not because they weren't nice. I really had no idea what I was looking for. Cringing, I grabbed the last hanger and flung it to my bed. "Did he say what he wanted?"

"King Aswell?" Ruenella's brow puckered, as if she had trouble understanding why I didn't know everything already. "He wants to see you."

"Well, isn't that nice of him to show up and assume I wanted to see him," I muttered sarcastically as I yanked the white sundress off the hanger.

"Come on," Ruenella's voice smoothly rolled out as she wistfully clasped her hands in front of her. "Don't you think it's sweet he's here? He's smitten with you."

I shot her a piercing look. "There is nothing about this arrangement that is sweet for me."

Ruenella's smile straightened. "I'll help you get dressed." She reached for my nightgown as soon as I slipped it over my head and hung it back up for me. By the time I had my dress on, she had already produced a brush and white velvet hair tie.

I sat at my vanity, and she quickly went to work, pulling my hair back into a long fishtail braid. "I don't know how you aren't excited about this," she gushed with a smile so large, you'd think all her dreams were coming true. "King Aswell is so handsome, and respected. You'll be queen and live on one of the most beautiful islands." She let out a dreamy sigh while she wrapped the velvet tie around the end of my braid.

"On one hand, it doesn't feel real." I stared at my reflection in my vanity mirror, wondering why he'd want to marry me when I had done nothing to win his affection.

"On the other hand, it's not how I pictured my life." My lashes fluttered slightly, and I fought to still them. It took so much strength, all I had left for a voice was a whisper, "I always thought I would get to make my own choices about getting married, and where I would live."

Her smile faded into a quarter smile. "So, you're not scared. Just not excited?"

I avoided her question. Instead forcing credence into my declaration, "We've stepped back into the Stone Age with these backroom marriage deals."

As I studied my reflection, I saw a woman who had grown up comfortably. This was the first time I recalled ever being asked to do anything to help my father. I had always been provided for. Maybe I should have felt important, knowing the fate of a country resided entirely in my actions. That wasn't the case at all. I felt an abandonment of myself. I was giving up on finding happiness and true love. My mind rewound to Reeves; his voice echoed in my head, "*Wait for true love ...*" Even though I'd never experienced love before, I was convinced love wasn't the main emotion I had for King Aswell.

I was also beginning to see Father as an obstacle to my own happiness. I loved him dearly, faults and all. I bit down into my bottom lip, remembering my childhood. He seemed always to pressure me to be someone I wasn't. My parents barely tolerated me spending all my time outside, and forever encouraged me to care about the arts, traveling and all things royal. I tried it all for them. I wanted so desperately to feel their affection, but even after all these things I'd done for them, it was never enough.

Now, they were literally expecting me to sign away my prospects of any future happiness, with no regards for what I wanted. But would that even be enough? What would I be forced into next while property of King Aswell? It could domino into one thing after the next. I would never be doing anything *I* wanted to do. Something must give. I highly suspected it wasn't going to be Father's pride. If I didn't stand up for myself sooner or later, it was never going to end. I blew out my frustrated breath as I slapped some fresh powder on my face. It was spotty and not blended even the slightest, but it would have to do. Maybe if I'm lucky my appearance might scare King Aswell away. I giggled, wishing so much my silly thoughts would come true.

"There she is!" Father extended an arm toward the grand staircase as both men observed my descent. Father wore his long-tailed red and gold coat, the one he normally reserved for formal military events. If this whole arrangement didn't already feel like a sham, his presentation made me ill. "Isn't she beautiful?" He trumpeted so loudly his voice echoed against the cathedral style ceilings.

I put on my best happy-to-be-here fake grin as I approached them. "Good morning." Before I could say anything else, Father ushered me forward, almost pushing me out of the door. "Come, Erralee. King Aswell has asked for your company. We don't want to keep him waiting. I have arranged for you two to go on a drive," he exclaimed with an enormous smile, but I knew that smile wasn't for me. If I had looked hard enough, I would have seen dollar signs on each corner of his lips. "You can show him our countryside while you get to know each other."

"I, ah." I held my chest in pause, as I wasn't ready to leave. I hadn't had breakfast, and everything was making me flustered. "What's the rush?"

"The driver is waiting." Father's hand found the small of my back and forcefully pushed me toward King Aswell, causing me to stumble forward. Being treated this way was humiliating, as if I were a puppet. Father was acting ridiculous. *Seriously straight out of the ancient times!*

"Perhaps we can stop for brunch?" King Aswell stepped forward, his eyes finding mine and softly pleading for understanding. Though he was dressed more casually today, without his royal cape, he was still in full black. Black still wasn't his color. His ominous vibe returned, and I felt as if a shadow fell over me. "Is there somewhere you'd like to eat?" His eyes paced over my face, studying me.

Father didn't like me to dine in town unless it was for his ratings. The only diner was a bit of a dive place, and it was "too common for people like us." With his recent actions, I was at the point where I didn't care anymore what Father wanted, or his forced etiquette. I'd walk down Main Street while hogging a pink hotdog with the mustard dripping off my chin. "That would be lovely," I replied loudly enough for Father to hear. "I'm quite hungry."

"Alright." Father clasped his hands in front of him, pointing toward the exit. "Have a nice time."

With Father's eyes locked on me, I didn't have anywhere to go but out the door. My foot was barely over the threshold when the door slammed behind us. I glanced back, doing my best to stay positive. I wasn't trying to be difficult, but I had nothing to say to King Aswell. This whole date was so awkward, and the only thing I could come up with was an apology. "I'm sorry if this looks extreme." I laced my fingers together, feeling the need to hold onto something. "My Father has never acted like this."

"Don't apologize. I have had many talks with him. I can assure you that I understand his position, and I don't fault you for it. He's under a great deal of stress. Which, I hope I can assist him with." He smiled at me in a way that was more genuine than anything, but I didn't want to see that. I didn't want to be the solution to anyone's problems other than my own. He motioned to the motorcade, waiting for us with my security car, and his car behind the royal cruiser.

I searched for Weston, panic seeding in my chest. If he was here, I'd at least have someone to secretly roll my eyes at. I found him sitting in the driver's seat of the cruiser, elbow out the open window, staring forward. He always found a way to be there for me. His gaze never wavered as we walked to the car, but he saw me. Always my protector, and I felt better as I climbed inside. Without being signaled, Weston started the car and drove forward.

"I brought a book I wanted to show you." King Aswell leaned forward and dug into a leather pouch. I hadn't even realized he'd had a bag with him. Then again, I was doing everything I could to avoid looking at him. It wasn't even his looks that I avoided, but it's as if every ounce of my soul was fighting to stop this, and since I had no control over where I was going, my only choice was where I laid my eyes. He pulled out a large picture book and slid it over to me.

"A book." I forced myself to grin. I didn't want to waste the effort to tell him I wasn't one of those people who liked to read.

"It's a collection of art by one of my friends. He has painted many of the landscapes in my home. I thought you might want to familiarize yourself with his style. If you would allow it, I would love for him to paint you someday."

I opened the cover and fanned through the first few pages. My governess had drilled art history into my core ever since I was a child. I was able to recognize the impressionist style, but I wasn't thrilled. "I don't know if painting portraits is something people do much anymore." I tried to sound as if I was contemplating more than looking for a way out of posing for a portrait. "Doesn't it make more sense to use a camera?"

"You don't like it?" His eyes traced my face, but he didn't sound disappointed. If anything, he seemed intrigued.

"Does it seem like a waste of time when a camera is more efficient? Not to mention all the different editing programs. You could have a picture that looks like it was painted, but in half of the time."

"But is it really the same?" He rubbed his chin before tacking on, "To me, art is half the process."

I shivered. Nothing he said, or did, brought goosebumps to dot my arm. The air was chilly. In the bustle of getting kicked out of my house, I hadn't had time to grab a coat. I wrapped my arms in front of me and wished for a warm coffee. "I could stop for that brunch you offered," I said, forcing a pleasant smile.

"Where would you like to go?" His salt and pepper brows snapped up to his hairline. "You know your little town best."

"The diner on Main Street is the only place there is." I leaned forward, speaking to Weston. "Do you think you can take us to the diner?"

He stole a glance at me in the rearview mirror. An amused spark in the corner of his eye caught my attention. Obviously, he could see how much I was forcing this. "I can call ahead, and we can pick it up and take you to the country for a picnic? That way you avoid making a public scene."

Even though this wasn't his date, sweet Weston understood what made me happy and tried to make this situation bearable. "I'd love—"

"A princess can't eat outside," King Aswell cut me off in answer to Weston. "The bugs are terrible this time of year."

I lowered my lashes, staring down at my feet. "You're right. What was I thinking?" I stifled a whimper while I internally begged for help. *Is this really going to be my life? I have no voice.*

"Perhaps, we can still order ahead, and take it to go," Weston rebutted with an eye on King Aswell in the rearview mirror. "Little towns are awfully gossipy, and you wouldn't get much time to chat."

King Aswell angled his chin sharply toward me and placed a hand over his mouth, concealing it as he spoke in a hushed voice. "Does your help always talk to you like they have a voice in what you do?"

"Oh, this is Weston." I waved my hand dismissively, fully understanding how this might not be seen as appropriate. "He's my personal guard and knows me well. He's just looking out for us." I motioned to the front seat, where Weston had appeared to slouch way down in his driver's seat. "I think it's a great idea to grab the food and eat it while we drive." *Not as pleasant as a picnic, but a compromise I was willing to make to avoid a public scene.*

King Aswell opened his mouth wide, but closed it before he spoke. Then he opened it again, saying, "Very well. If you insist, that's what you want."

"It's just easier to have a private conversation, and since that's what we are trying to do . . . You know, get to know each other." I lifted one shoulder in pause, as tension pooled in my upper back. *Why is this so hard?*

"It's fine." He curtly nodded, then tacked on, "What would you like to talk about?"

"Well." I blew out a long breath, while I pulled up every-thing, I already knew about him, which wasn't much. We already discussed his boring books and museums. He af-firmed he doesn't like the outdoors . . . I pulled my lips to one side, digging deep for a topic, but the only thing that kept reeling back was the question of "why." Father would have said it was rude, but I wasn't afraid of Father, so I pressed, "I know I already asked you why you chose me. I'm still a little curious as to why you would even want to agree to a partnership with my father. Aside from gaining a wife. I'm sure you can easily find someone without having to extend your military. This war is brutal. Why are you even getting involved?"

He wasn't one to fidget. He sat straight. Kept his gaze fixed and spoke directly. "This war needs to end. It's been unfair from the start, as everyone knows your father never had the means to even come close to defending himself. It's an attempt at a totalitarian takeover. They want to control his land, and because your father is weak, they think they can take it. It's unjust. I'm not one to sit back and let unjust things just happen."

I had never heard an explanation of the war from any viewpoint other than my father's boastful side. Of course, my father never admitted he was weak. It was interesting to hear what others truly thought of him. Humbling.

I leaned to the side, shifting my weight as Weston sharply pulled the car over on the side of the road, parking. "We are here!" He announced, while pushing open his door. "Just wait one moment, and I'll be back with your food."

"Good." King Aswell stated, shuffling in his seat as he appeared to be looking for something. From the front seat pocket, he pulled out another book. My eyes grew wide. *This can't happen again. Didn't I already explain I wasn't much of a reader?*

"While we wait for his return, I wanted to show you one of my favorite poetry collections. Most of these are in French, but I'm actually quite fluent . . ." He kept talking, but my mind ran off, completely lost to this conversation. *Help! He's talking about his boring books again!* I fought every urge I had to pound on the window and cry out. Somehow, I managed to maintain perfect princess etiquette and smile as we peered at the book together, each and *every* word-crusted page.

Seven

Reeves

I didn't even need to adjust my line of vision; I had honed a sixth sense of knowing she was there. Like an adamant stray cat, she kept coming back. Only today, I wasn't so quick to push her away. Instead, I threw on a clean t-shirt and my jean jacket. Then I headed out the backdoor with extra pep in my stride. A smile that had been there most of the morning only inflated on my face as I hurried out. I didn't want to seem too eager. As I approached her, I slowed, pretending to accidentally stumble across her.

"Hey, you!" I called out to her, not as forcefully as the last time I had done this. Today she wore a white sundress, and her hair was tied back. Her entire look was more casual than last night, but the mere sight of her sent an unfamiliar zing to my gut. She didn't banter back as I had expected. Instead, she turned her chin away from me, hiding her eyes.

Was this a game?

She wouldn't have come to *my* field if she didn't want to see me. Right?

I'll never understand women, but that won't stop me from trying. "How are you?" I asked, in the friendliest tone I'd used since I had been discharged. This was the first time I wanted to have a conversation, and she wasn't making it easy. "Are you still sad about what happened?"

"What happened?" She snapped out, still not looking my way.

I scratched an imaginary itch on my cheek. "Are you still getting married?"

"Yep." She popped the p on the end of the word and then pursed her lips. The clouds had rolled in, shading what was usually the sunniest spot in the field, and she had her arms wrapped across her chest with obvious goosebumps dotting them.

I removed my jacket, wincing when I got a whiff. It could have benefitted from a good washing, but that didn't stop me from draping it on her bare shoulders. Her lashes fluttered before she locked her gaze on me. "What was that for?"

Shifting my weight from one foot to the other, I downplayed my gesture. "You looked cold."

"I didn't have time to grab a coat this morning." She bristled with shallow breaths. "I was pushed out with *that man*. When I returned home, I was too upset to face my Father to go inside and get one."

"That man?" I hmphed, thinking that sounded good for me. There was no way she was getting married with that attitude.

"What am I supposed to call him?" she asked facetiously, her lip pouting out.

I swallowed back a laugh. Maybe I should have left her alone, but she was strangely adorable when she groused. "I think the proper term is fiancé." I said it, both to tease her and to pry. I wasn't in the position to ask about her status, but inside I was dying to know.

"Not yet." She held up an interjecting finger. "I have six more days."

"Is that so?" My heart ticked up a notch, sounding an alarm. "Then what?"

"I have to make my decision." She snorted after her random response, before adding, "Even though the decision was already made, and not by me."

I raised an inquiring brow. "Or?"

"Or I assume he gives up and goes home. He said he wasn't going to wait forever. I'm not worth forever." She sighed as if letting go of a fantasy. "It's not a fairytale. I only get one week."

"He can't be that bad." I wasn't trying to talk her into liking him. It was my cunning way to get her to think about all his less attractive qualities. If I could only get her to stall for the week, that wouldn't be too hard. Then he'd go home.

"He's dreadfully boring," she moaned without needing more coaxing. "Aside from the fact that I could go fishing with his nose."

I chuckled, looking down my own nose for a quick size check. I didn't see any minnows nipping at it, so I presumed that was a good sign. "Do you like to fish?"

"Nah, or I would see that as an asset then." She tried to be serious with her reply, but as soon as the word was out, she sputtered out a small giggle.

"So, Mr. Dreadfully-boring king isn't your type." I plopped down next to her, stretching my legs out in front. I'd wasted enough time on this topic. Unless I was trying to make her cry again—which I wasn't—I needed to move the conversation. I tossed a casual look in her direction. "Tell me who is?"

She pulled her legs up, wrapped her arms around them, and rested her chin on top as she stared forward out into the prairie. "For me, it's about finding someone I can be myself with. I feel so much pressure to look perfect, and say the right things to him. A lot of that is because of my father, but I can also tell King Aswell expects high standards. And he's smart." She flicked her hand in a gesture toward me. "He talks about his libraries and museums, and not only do I find those things claustrophobicing, but I don't think I'm intelligent enough to have anything to add on those topics."

My lips pulled up tight at the edges as I fought the urge to tease her. She was already being hard on herself, but I couldn't let it go. "I can see that."

"You can?"

"I do. Especially since claustrophobic*ing* is not a real word."

"Either is irregardless, but it's now in the dictionary, so I figured I could use made up words, too." Her voice fell into more of a whimper at the end. "Sometimes the real words aren't strong enough to describe my state of emotions."

I had been trying to get her to laugh, not upset her further. Of course, I didn't think she was uneducated or anything. She went quiet, looking forward as if something interesting was in the distance, keeping her attention. I followed her gaze, but all I saw was the prairie, including a single white butterfly fluttering in the distance. As beautiful as it was, it wasn't enough to warrant staring at it for this long. Suddenly, I was curious about her. If she found powerful kings uninteresting, why did she come here? "Can I ask what about this field makes you keep coming back?"

Without pause, she quipped back, "Can I ask you what it was about this field that made you steal it from me?"

"Whoa, now that's not fair." I pushed out a friendly elbow and tapped hers. "We both know I didn't steal anything. I bought it honestly, and I didn't even know about you." Still trying to make her smile, I tack on a joke, "had I known about you, I might have negotiated a discount."

"Sorry." She blew out a frustrated breath as her dark lashes lowered. "I'm having a hard time dealing with change."

"It's alright." I kept my expressionless face. "You have a lot to consider."

"That's the thing because I don't have anything to consider. I don't get a say in any of this. It's an impossible choice." She remained still, rambling on. "It's either do what I want and maybe be happy and countless people die. My country goes to ruins, which means I wouldn't ever forgive myself. I wouldn't be happy anyway. *Or* get married to a miserable man and pray everything is fixed, so at least I can feel good about that." Her eyes snapped back at me. Despair was blaring through her irises. "So, no, I don't get a say. All I have is a few days. I can't stand being around my father right now. King Aswell is always swarming around, trying to get to know me. I literally have no autonomy at the castle, so if you don't mind," her voice softened as if she struggled to hold back a quiver, "I'd like to spend my last week of freedom here."

Unsure of how to help her, I was increasingly growing more concerned about her situation. It didn't seem right that King Aswell would insist on marrying someone who didn't appear to like him, even if she was a princess. No guy wanted that marriage. At least no guy I knew. Guys don't ask for much. A happy wife, who smiled when he came home, maybe a kid or two. Having a wife who despises you, well, that wouldn't be on anyone's short list.

What is King Aswell really up to?

The hair on the back of my neck stood up as I grew increasingly more protective of her. It was clear she was doing everything she could to avoid breaking down. Even though the whole thing was beyond my control, it wasn't lost on me that she was here with me now. I was compelled to comfort her. "What do you want to do?"

"Nothing." She let out a shaky breath. "Just be here until I can't."

"Maybe you're overreacting?" I lowered my voice. "You're getting married. He's not taking you to jail."

"It's hard to explain." She tucked a stray hair behind her ear, but the light wind instantly released it. She was quite stunning, even if she wasn't smiling. Her high cheekbones completed her heart-shaped face, which made a perfect frame for those almond-shaped eyes. Maybe King Aswell was just after beauty? I could see that. Afterall, Erralee said he was into art. She was clearly a breathing masterpiece.

"On the surface, it makes sense to me. It shouldn't be hard. People say love is a choice. Maybe I should choose to love him?" A crease of disappointment crept between her eyes, and she pulled at the wild grass, making a neat pile in her lap. Clearly it was a fidget, and I doubted she realized she was doing it as she went on, "But I feel so deeply in my soul that it's wrong. Even though it's for a good cause, it's a fraud. It feels like it's one of those things which must play out in a long life where I can look back, in hindsight and point to those people who pressured me on this path. Then I could say, 'see there. That was wrong. You forced me on a path that was bad for me.' The irony is I must waste myself to prove that point."

It was hard for me to listen to her. She had lost the fire in her eyes she had only a couple of days earlier. That's what scared me. If she'd lost this much of herself in a few days, what would be left after a lifetime of living in a forced marriage?

She was silent after that, and I got up and could have left her alone with her thoughts, but something shifted inside of me. She had six days, and I wasn't going to waste one. "Come with me." I reached my hand out, waiting for her.

"Where?"

"Where?" I echoed, not because I was playing coy, but because I had no idea myself. I was flying by the seat of my pants, and I didn't want her sitting here sulking about Mr. Boring. "It's a surprise."

She tapped her finger to her chin, as her gaze flickered back at me. "Give me a hint."

"I don't know any." I cleared my throat, "I mean, hmm, wait a second." My brain raced through all the things we could do in the field. We could walk, we could run, we could skip, okay now I sounded like a nursery rhyme. She said she liked excitement.

Aha! I had an idea.

Eight

Princess Erralee

"I'm not climbing up there." I eyed the jagged rock tower overlooking the small creek. I wasn't against hiking. I rather enjoyed a good walk, but this was a straight up rock-climbing situation, and I was in a dress.

Let's face it. Even if I wasn't in a dress, I still didn't want to climb that.

"I'll pull you up." Reeves' sun-bronzed arm reached out to me. He had the kind of arms that told the truth of his hard work with carved sinewy ripples and stained in scars too deep to heal. It wasn't his arms that were hard not to stare at, but his prosthetic hand. He hadn't ever mentioned it. Not that he owed me any explanation, but I wondered what it felt like. Could he even tell if I was holding it? I trusted he knew what he was doing. It didn't slow him down. Was I allowed to ask about his hand? He must have read my mind because he added, "It's safe. You aren't going to break it."

"It's quite fine. Thanks anyway, but I'll pass." Convinced solid ground was the best place for me, I stood, unmoved. "It's rather nice down here."

"I listened to you complain about your boring old bookish fiancé. You claimed you liked to do fun things." He waved his hand, inviting me over. "Prove it."

"This isn't fun." I steeled my jaw, half serious, and half wanting to flirt. Something about how his eyes glistened back at me brought the butterflies to life in my gut. "It's reckless."

"Look at it this way." He gestured in a teasing manner. "If you die, you don't have to get married."

"Well, when you put it that way," I joked, pretending to hop right in line with him, but then took a step back after he laughed. He was crazy if he thought I would skitter up after him on that thing.

"Come on." Reeves found a crevice in the rock and pulled himself up.

"No," I called after him, not adding anything else because I always understood that when faced with life-threatening situations, no is a full sentence. He climbed up another level, smirking as if he was having the best time ever.

"Suit yourself," he called down. "Stay there and be *bored*. It'll be good practice for your marriage."

I wasn't what you'd call a competitive person, but his words hit a nerve. One that had been niggling at me for the last few days. I didn't want to waste my life between stone walls, reading books, not living my life. This might be my last real chance to experience fun. Against my better judgment, I abandoned my good sense, slipped off my heeled sandals, and stepped forward. "You'll help me?" I called up as I stepped into the crevice.

"Sure, step in the same places I do." He stalled, waiting for me to catch up. "I climbed this thing a dozen times already. It's completely safe."

I wrapped my fingers around a jutting rock and lifted my foot up a level.

"Not that one," he quickly cautioned. "That one is wobbly."

Not sure if he was teasing, or being extra careful, I took his advice, and shimmied over an extra rock, I had to stretch way to the side, and it pulled my calf muscle into a deep stretch. *This is absurd! If my father saw me do this, he'd blow smoke out of his ears.* Which in a way, made it even more fun. My heart ramped up a notch, and I steadied my gaze on Reeves. He was about halfway up, which meant . . . if I fell, I'd also fall about halfway down.

I exhaled through slit lips, raising my foot the smallest level up, as I had gotten relatively good at spotting the little crevices between the rocks to put my feet in. If I looked up, it really wasn't scary. I could hear Reeves taking heavy measured breaths above me, and in an odd way that made me feel better.

I wasn't the only one struggling not to die.

"Grab my hand." Reeves was at the top, reaching his prosthetic back to me. I had no idea how I'd already made it as it hadn't been more than a couple of minutes, but it felt like an hour. I carefully reached out and wrapped my hand around his prosthetic palm. It scratched against mine, but I was impressed as he pulled me up with one swift, strong motion.

It was a tad windy as I crawled forward and found a nice spot in the center to sit. I was in awe of the view. "I can't believe I've never been up here before," I said, seeing almost the entire countryside, including my home, from here.

"I can," Reeve teased, his smile stretching wide across his face, revealing his perfect teeth. "With the way I had to twist your arm, I'm surprised I got you up here now."

"I'm more of a bottom of the valley, girl," I mused, while still feeling the heavy beat of my heart in my head. "Is this where you come to hang out?"

"I wouldn't call it a hang out." He tottered towards the edge, calling back, "Come on."

I figured he wanted me to see the view, but he got so close to the edge, his toes were hanging over. "You aren't going to push me, are you?" I half-joked. Still too nervous to stand, I crawled forward on my hands and knees.

His silvery blue eyes sparked with mischief. "No, we go down together."

"Excuse me?" I halted, not at all enjoying his tone. I slowly stood but stayed more than an arm's length away from the edge.

He nodded over the edge, and my gaze followed, finding that it was a *long* way down to the creek at the bottom. "Oh no!" I backed away after solving his riddle. "I'm not jumping. I'll climb down the way we came."

"You said you have six days to have fun." He extended his open hand out toward me, his eyes glistened daringly at me. "Let's start now."

Almost every part of me wanted to back away and go down how I had come, but one tiny part inside betrayed me with the loudest vote. Uttering, "someday you'll be eighty and looking back at your life, and all your memories. You'll want to remember the rush of this moment. If I died, well, then that would work out too."

Completely out of character, I took a confirming step forward as I squealed in my mind. Reeve's lips curled more with each inch I moved. "You can do this," he urged. "Consider it a puddle of water. Completely harmless."

This time he offered me his real hand, and I savored how his fingers laced through mine. His grip was sturdy and secure. My gaze fell to my hand holding onto his, and I memorized the way it felt. Something told me I'd want to remember that, too.

I crept forward, finding my path—

"Don't look down," his words of caution broke my thoughts.

I wiggled my toes to the edge until I felt them curl at the tips. "How do I know where to jump?"

"Jump forward and don't let go." He squeezed my hand tighter, and I curled my fingers safely around his.

My nerves began to unravel even more as I went through the logistics of the next few minutes. "Do I close my eyes or keep them open?"

"That's up to you."

"Oh." My breath quivered out, and I closed my eyes, squeezing them tight. "I think I'm better off dying with eyes closed."

"No, this is the opposite of dying. This is where you live." He squeezed my hand again, and it sent a shock right through me. "Remember, we go down together."

"When is this going to be?" My eyes were still closed, and I doubted I would muster up the courage to jump without him having to pull me over. "How do I get over the fear?"

"You don't." His voice came out husky as if he'd suddenly recalled a bad memory. "When you think it's the *scariest* to jump . . . that's when you jump."

"That sounds like a terrible idea," I spat out, but then froze. We were standing on the edge of the cliff, toes hanging over enough that a strong wind could tip me over. Something told me Reeves was trying to teach me more than just how to jump. This was a living metaphor for my entire situation. I opened one eye, peeking back at him, his eyes hovered on me with such intensity, I understood he was trying to show me my strength. I looked down, and when my life didn't immediately flash before my eyes, I was oddly calmed. I took a deep breath, and squeezed his hand as hard as I could. There was no way I would let him ditch me now, and I stepped over the ledge.

I thought it would be gradual, like the descent on a swing, but I was wrong! Gravity was instant, plummeting me down. Filling my chest with adrenaline, I screamed as if my wails were capable of poofing out a parachute.

I plunged feet-first into the frigid water. The cold should have been disabling, but it was the opposite, sparking me more awake than I'd ever felt. Adrenaline ripped through my core, filling me until I couldn't contain it anymore, and a giant smile burst onto my face.

I squeezed Reeve's hand, and he surprised me by wrapping his free arm around my waist, pulling me into him as we kicked toward the surface. His hand on my waist instantly stole the last of my breath as being in his arms awakened a spark that seemed to have a magnetic force. Even underwater I felt the heat flush across my cheeks, and my heart hammered so fast I thought it would crash through the walls of my chest. I had nearly forgotten how to swim, but his strong kicks propelled us both to the surface.

When I broke out of the water, I gasped for air. Reeves shook his head, freeing his buzzed hair from much of the dripping water. We both trod water, but neither of us let go of the other. After more than a beat, he broke the silence. "You made it."

"I did," I huffed out as I continued to kick my feet fiercely.

I doubted his lips could curl anymore, but he managed an even bigger smile, as if it alone was proof of what we had braved. "I'm proud of you."

Although I continued to smile with my lips, there was a stirring in my heart that I hadn't felt before. It made my toes curl under. I held Reeve's gaze, neither one of us flinching or making even the slightest move to let go. The stirring swelled, filling my whole chest.

My eyes traced his face, noticing everything from his strong jawline to his eyes framed with several smile crinkles in the corners. I had the urge to memorize all the visible lines of his face as there was something rare about this moment being in his arms that made me feel alive.

He slowly ran his teeth over his bottom lip, then stilled and gazed at me the way I didn't even know I needed to be looked at. *Desire.* It's the way a man should look at a woman, and this was the first time it had ever happened to me, making my heart speed up.

I didn't even need to kick my legs to tread water, because it felt as if I was floating. His hand slid up, cupping the back of my neck, as I leaned closer. His gaze dropped to my lips and hovered. A mere second later, he shook his chin as if pulled from a trance and his gaze shot back to shore. Releasing my hand, he focused on land and called over his shoulder, "Let's swim back."

What just happened!

Stunned, I triple blinked as I stifled a disappointed sigh and swam. Back on the riverbank, his demeanor instantly changed. Where before, he had been reaching for my hand and holding me in the water. Now he seemed to do everything he could to avert eye contact. "That was intense." I breathed loudly, hoping to stir the conversation.

"Yeah," he muttered, keeping his gaze down, as he took his boots off one at a time, dumping the water out of them. Then he spent way too much time adjusting his pant legs into them. They were suctioned to his leg with nowhere to move, but it didn't stop him from fidgeting with it while he waited for me to catch up.

"I mean, it was amazing." I paced toward him, and smiled sweetly, hoping to rekindle that spark we just shared in the water.

"Glad you lived." He stared off in the distance the way we had come, murmuring, "My chores aren't going to do themselves. And your father's probably wondering where you are?"

If there was ever a way to kill a moment, it was to bring up my father. My heart instantly plummeted, and I checked the sky. The sun was setting, bringing in hues of burnt orange. It had to be near dinner time, and my absence would not go unnoticed. "You are probably right."

"Alright." He backed away, not giving me the chance to say a proper goodbye. "Have a good night." He waved, and spun on his heel, speeding off. If I'd hadn't known better, I'd think I made him uncomfortable. How he'd gone from almost kissing me, to acting scared of me was beyond me. *Did I do something wrong?*

Sloshing forward with a wet dress stuck to my skin like plastic wrap, I scurried back down the path to the castle. I had lost track of time, and was going to be late for dinner. Although we hadn't discussed it, I didn't doubt that life-of-the-party King Aswell would be a guest. Father would be livid if I was even a moment late. Halfway through the forest, Weston caught up to me, equally out of breath. With my gaze on the trail ahead and a lump of dread in my throat, I called out, "Are they looking for me?"

"Not yet," he hollered back. "I told them you were napping." A mischievous smile grew on his lips. "Course, I didn't tell them you were off swimming with some wild cowboy."

"I didn't see you!" I gasped, letting my hand fly to my chest.

"I keep my distance." He chuckled, showing the small chip in his eyetooth. The one he got when he accidentally slapped his face against a fence while running after a rogue frisbee I'd thrown at him when we were young. Our lives were so entwined, it was impossible for me to remember one stage of my life without him. Even now, I was not embarrassed he saw me with Reeves. If anything, I couldn't wait to tell him all about it. "You know I always protect you." His lips rolled in casually. "It looked likc you were having fun."

Sighing, as his words dared me to speak my truth, I never held back with Weston. "I did," I said wistfully. "I'm not even sure what happened, because I thought he was like this grumpy cowboy. Something about him switched ... Now he's . . ." I nodded as if moving my head would help me get the words out, "fun," I almost whispered, but instead said, "I feel as if I'm living a normal life when I'm with him."

"I'm glad. He seems like he'd be a good guy for you. You have a lot in common." He pushed a small bundle toward me. "I messaged Ruenella when I saw you jump over the edge. She ran and met me with dry clothes. If your father sees you like this, he'll have an aneurysm."

"Right." My gaze shifted to the bundle. We were in the middle of the forest, and I couldn't even see the road. Weston turned his back. I didn't waste time peeling out of my soaked dress. Then I rushed to unfold the silk fabric from the bundle and slipped into one of my finest dinner dresses. "Done," I announced while stepping back onto the path. "How much time do you think we have?"

"Put it this way," Weston's voice budded with urgency. "Run!"

Weston and I ran as if our lives depended on it, laughing like kids the whole way. Something about this day didn't feel real. Starting with the most awkward drive this morning, and then a complete one-eighty event of cliff diving with a man I had a growing attraction for. Now, I was running home . . . back to my destiny of dread.

As we tore through the front door, I forced myself to slow my steps into a more lady-like pattern, in case Father was nearby. Weston cased the foyer and whispered, "It's clear." He stood tall and astute as a royal guard should, and waved me in. "Hurry."

"I'm going upstairs to powder quickly. If Father comes looking, tell him I'll be right down." I hurdled the stairs two at a time, not stopping until I was in the bathroom. I threw powder on my face and outlined my eyes in mascara. I wasn't trying to impress anyone, just avoiding trouble. My hair was still braided and tied back as Ruenella had fixed it this morning. I didn't have time to mess with it. If I took it down, I'd need to shower to fix it. Thankfully the top layer had air dried from running in the wind. I prayed nobody would question the dampness underneath as I grabbed a wrap and covered the goosebumps on my shoulders.

In the dining room, I found Mother and Ruenella.

No Father.

No King Aswell.

The table was made up with places set for both, but their plates were still clean.

Instead of the festive spread of food I had expected, they were sipping root vegetable soup with half-hooded eyes. The only beverage set on the table was a pitcher of water. There wasn't even ice or lemon to garnish it. I slowed my steps and took my usual spot next to Mother. "Good evening," I said, not feeling chatty, but doing my best to have manners.

Mother hardly glanced at me, but that wasn't completely unusual for her. I shifted my gaze to my sister. "What's going on? Where's Father?"

She covered her mouth while she finished chewing. In a hushed voice, she stated matter-of-factly, "Eastbury Pines has been taken under siege. They had to call a meeting."

Alarm seeped into my chest while I did the math. That was the closest major city to us. "That's only a hundred miles away," I whispered, suddenly feeling ill. "Do we have troops on the ground yet? Are we going to stop it?"

"There aren't any troops left to move." Ruenella took a sip of her drink, and then tacked on, "Father is calling in air support. It'll have to do for now."

"Shh," Mother said sternly as if noticing our conversation for the first time. She'd clearly been in her own headspace.

"Let's not talk about war at the dinner table." She motioned to the soup crock in the center of the table. "Erralee, please help yourself. I've given the wait staff the night off to spend with family."

I wasn't the least bit hungry despite the fact I'd hadn't eaten since brunch with King Aswell. "I suppose you think this is my fault," I whispered. I didn't need to be blamed because the guilt had already encased my heart. This war could have been over if I hadn't been so stubborn.

"It is what it is," Mother's voice rolled out, lacking empathy.

I stared forward at my empty soup bowl, feeling as if it were a visual crossroads. I hadn't planned on the stakes getting higher, or the war this close to home. A bulge crept into my throat as I slid my chair back, the legs loudly rubbing, attracting Mother's stern gaze. Before she could ask, I said, "I'll talk to King Aswell tomorrow."

Nine

Reeves

Back in the truck on another trip to town for a new stupid pipe fitting. I was beginning to sound like my old man, but they didn't make stuff like they used to. Stupid plastic junk was already cracked. I didn't even get it out of the package, and I could tell it wasn't right. On top of that, I couldn't stop yawning, but it wasn't because of my lack of coffee. I was up all night, tossing with my thoughts all garbled up. Mostly I kept picturing Erralee in the water. It was an absurdity to even consider, but I'd seen that look before, and she'd clearly wanted me to kiss her.

I couldn't do it.

I wanted to kiss her.

My insides froze.

My brain froze.

My *everything* jammed up.

Even as awkward as it was trying to pretend we didn't almost kiss, I'm glad we didn't. I'd suffer dearly for that later when she moved along to get married. Somedays I could barely do life. The last thing I needed was to survive a heartbreak.

And what is up with this small town? I forced my brain into a change of subject. For only a few thousand people, they did an awful lot of gathering in the middle of town, which forced me into finding a parking space more elusive than the Bermuda triangle. I settled on parking in an alley off Main Street. Apparently, some sort of a flea market plugged up all the paved roads.

People meandered from one end of the street down to the other. Farmers with produce stands, women selling knitted shower cap looking thingys in every size, people with used books and pottery. I was pretty sure it was town clean-out-your-junk day. I dodged a woman pulling a wagon piled full of kids. She had so many children, and not one of them had a decent haircut. It looked as if she had a wagon load of mops.

Not having planned on this today, I swiped my forehead, anxiety inflating in my chest. People everywhere being way too people-y. This was different from the festival the other night. It seemed so much more disorganized, and without the music to focus on, my unease grew.

I could come back . . .

I don't really *need* water to live anyway.

I'll be fine for a few days.

I *need* to get out of here.

I tried whistling to calm my nerves. The only thing that I succeeded in doing, was making me look like a crazy person. I turned on my heel, but I immediately had to dodge hordes of people. I got mixed up and started walking in the wrong direction. Panic filled my chest. The ground appeared to wobble, threatening to open up and suck me in. I was sinking!

Battlefield memories of being trapped circled my head, and I got dizzy. I dodged the crowd left, and veered right, only to be met with kids laughing in my ear, and chatter swirling all around. I found it rather odd that people were still going about in merriment with the war looming not far away. Then again, the war had gone on for so long, they more than likely had gone numb to it.

Marching band music wafted in the air, reminding me of a high school spirit song. It was an unrecognizable tune that did everything it could to throw me off balance.

I was losing my mind.

Stumbling backward, trying to right my direction, I plowed into a lady carrying a large, flat basket. Her basket flipped, and dozens of long-stem roses tumbled to her feet.

"Sorry," I muttered, immediately taking a knee and collecting them.

"Reeves," a voice I didn't know floated above my head. "That's you, right? I recognized the hand."

Of course, she did. It was impossible to hide it. Once people heard my story, they acted like I was public property. I lifted my heavy eyelids. A woman met my gaze, but I couldn't place her. "Uh, do I know you?" I tipped my hat up and let my eyes rake over her auburn curls.

"Francine." She paused, smiling back at me as if that should have rung a bell. It didn't, and my head was swelling with a headache each second longer I had to stand there.

"Elliot," she added. Smiling even wider.

"E-Elliot?" I stammered, feeling the sweat immediately slap on my back. "You're Frank's widow." My vision suddenly split into dual screens. I was still staring at her, but a figment of my closest comrade flashed in front of my eyes. Startled, I took a step back. I clenched my eyelids and rubbed my palm over my eyes, but still I saw his face. Turning my head, I tried to remove the image, but it followed me like a mirage in the desert. It would only be a moment, and I guessed I'd hear his voice. My feet tingled, ready to flee. *I need to get out of here.*

Thankfully her soft voice centered me back to the present day. "I am."

I panted out, breathing as if it was the first real breath I'd taken in the last five minutes. "I'm so sorry for your loss," I fumbled, as I stacked the last of the roses back into her basket, patting my hand on top, steadying them.

"Thank you." Her lashes lowered thoughtfully before she said, "And, how are you?"

Clearing my throat, I managed, "I'm here." I motioned to the flowers, desperate to get the conversation off me. "Are you vending here?"

"Yes." She shifted the weight of the basket into her other arm. "It's a side job I added to help with Little Frank's schooling."

"Wait a second." My brows knitted together, already hating the way this conversation was going. "You're selling these to pay for your boy's education?"

"For now." She pulled her lips tight. "I didn't have the heart to switch his schools on top of everything else he's been through. It's only once a month and that extra money helps so much."

How much could she possibly make selling roses once a month? Seems implausible that she'd make enough for anything but a tank of gas. She must have been desperate to bother. My gaze scanned the sidewalk, seeing many kids but no mini-Frank. "And where is he now?"

She hiked a thumb over her shoulder, pointing north. "He's with a neighbor while I work."

My back molars ground together. I couldn't comprehend how weird this was, running into my fallen friend's widow on the street, nearly begging for money. I yanked my money clip out of my pocket and peeled off a few bills. "What do they sell for? I'll take the whole bundle so you can go home and spend time with your boy."

"Ah, heaven's no." She took a step back, flashing her palm. "It's fine. I usually sell out in three or four hours."

"No," I sternly affirmed, taking my entire cash wad, placing it in her hand. I didn't have the words to tell her that Elliot had my back the entire time. War buddies. He'd saved me more than once. He was the *only* reason I was standing here instead of him. "It's really not much, but maybe you can make a memory with little Frank."

Her lashes fluttered, fighting back tears, as her fingers curled around the cash.

I reached toward her basket. "I'll take those flowers off your hands."

"It's one hundred roses." She raised a skeptical brow. "What are you going to do with them?"

"I must be assured you don't stay to sell them and actually go home."

She released the basket. I was rather surprised by how heavy it was, as I slid the basket on to my arm, shifting the weight. She reached out and cupped my cheek in her hand, holding it there while she paused. "Thank you—"

"Don't," I cut her off with a whisper, doing my best not to be rude. This conversation was dragging on more than I would have liked. It wasn't that I didn't appreciate her, or Frank. It was too much of my past bleeding into my present. Nobody in this little town was supposed to know me. If I didn't get away from her soon, more memories would come flooding back, and I couldn't have that. I backed away from her, and waved goodbye. "I'm not going to keep you."

She flashed her hand up in a wave and turned on her heel, heading the opposite direction. Then I pivoted, not used to this giant foliage on my arm, and for the second time tonight crashed this stupid basket. *Clearly, this thing needs caution lights.*

"Ferschimmelt!" a voice called out.

"Excuse me." I steadied my basket again and successfully held the roses stacked on top. My lips parted at the sight of

Erralee standing before me, wearing another yellow dress and a sun hat. Even if she hadn't been an actual princess, she looked like one. Her hair flowed down her shoulders, framing her perfect feminine posture. Her lips were flawlessly pouty, the perfect place to drop a kiss. *Whoa, what!* I forced my eyes to cement on hers, away from her kissable lips.

"Hey, Reeves." She offered a sheepish grin, her cheeks spiking a blush that matched her already redder-than-usual nose.

"H-Hey." I fumbled, still restacking the roses, which by now had started to tatter with some of the petals peeling back. A few stray petals even fell to the ground by my feet. "What did you call me?"

"Oh, it wasn't a name. It's Yiddish." She waved dismissively. "I'm not allowed to swear, but I've collected a handful of funny words that feel good to blurt out."

I blinked, both amazed I'd bumped into her in this sea of people, while also stunned that she'd be here in the first place. "Um, that's interesting. What does it mean?"

"Oh." She flicked her hand in a ladylike manner. "It's a wrinkly vegetable, but nobody knows that. It's fun to say." She smiled daringly and urged, "Try it."

"Try saying ferchim . . . "

"It's *fer shim melt* and say it with conviction." She curled her hand into a fist and shook it playfully in front of her face.

"Ferschimmelt." I enunciated each syllable, feeling proud I could get that word out in one breath.

She offered a humorous scowl. "You can say it louder than that."

I checked behind me. Yep, people were still everywhere, and likely to think I was nuts. I had no idea how she was getting me to do this silly thing, but I proceeded to practically shout, "Fershimmelt!"

Placing her hand over her mouth, she concealed a giggle. "That was much better."

"I'm surprised I ran into you here." I gestured toward the street. "I didn't think flea markets would be your thing. No open fields for you to nap in—" *I stopped before I mentioned rock climbing. That would just be awkward. Why do my toes curl just being near her? I'm sure it has nothing to do with our almost kiss yesterday.*

Her lips pulled into an uncomfortable grimace. "I'm making the last of my goodbye rounds."

"Goodbye?" My brow dropped as suddenly the reddened tip of her nose made sense. She had obviously been crying. By the look of dread in her eyes, I guessed it was something horrific. "Say what?" I fumbled, hoping to rewind her words.

Her lips tightened before she leaked out, "I ah, am officially accepting King Aswell's proposal tonight." She raised both brows in what should have been a look of excitement, but the inflections in her eyes confessed her lies.

She was close to tears, and so was I!

I thought she had five more days!

"Oh, man." I ran a hand along my forehead, feeling a tad feverish. "Are you sure you want to say that so soon? Maybe you need to get to know him for a while. Marriage is a big deal," my voice squeaked. Such a travesty. I needed to work on that.

Her shoulder raised, faking she didn't care, but despair swirled in her eyes. She was not convinced yet. I still had hope. *I have a chance to change her mind!* Now, I needed a plan. My gaze dropped to the sidewalk, until I was reminded of the giant basket of roses in my hand. It was so perfect I almost yelped. "Here." I pushed the whole basket forward, pulling one side of my lips into a half grin. "I ah, got you roses. I planned this whole surprise for you, but haha, it looks like you busted me."

"You did?" Her gaze dropped to the basket. "That's awfully sweet, but why would you do that?"

Why would I do that? I drummed my fingers on the side of my leg as I mulled this over. That's a good question. No, it's a great question that deserves a good answer. "Er, isn't it obvious?"

"No." She shook her head back and forth while still staring at the flowers. "Those are red roses. Usually, you give red to someone you—"

"Love," I cut her off, unsure why I just spit out the L word. I mean, I definitely wasn't going to be busting that out any time soon. "Right." I waved my free hand gingerly over the basket. "This wasn't really about *love*. It's more of a convenience of color," I rambled. "It's more of an I-was-thinking-about-you sort of thing."

"That's really sweet." She pinned a confused line between her brows. "I don't think I can accept them, though. Out of respect for my situation, and all."

This can't be happening! How can I be out of time? Oh, wait . . . she said she was accepting the offer *tonight. I still had today!* I checked behind her. She appeared to be alone. "Ah, are you here with *him* now?"

"No," her words tumbled out, laced with relief. "I snuck out by myself. There have been many closed-door meetings at the castle, so I waited for one."

"We need to go somewhere alone," I accidentally mumbled out loud when I thought I was only thinking it.

Her chin took an angled stance. "Pardon me?"

"Oh, I mean, ah, if you're *leaving*." I clasped my hands in front of me and leaned a measure toward her. "You should let me do something nice for you."

"I should be getting back to the castle soon. It's quite a walk." Her gaze skirted to the side, and she dropped her voice. "I don't want anyone to discover I snuck out without my security."

"You don't have your guard," I rushed to echo as this was the best news ever! If she was alone, then I could offer a ride home and get more time with her. "How about I take you home!" I blurted out eagerly, then immediately dropped my tone, "I mean, I don't think it's safe for you to be off wandering around without security. Plus, I can bring your roses too." Her eyes dropped to the basket again, and her lips pinched. Before she refused, I tacked on, "Consider them congratulations."

"Ah, okay." Her nervous gaze slid forward. "That might be okay."

"Perfect." I ushered her forward toward the alley where my truck was parked. "So right this way. It's not a royal chariot," I joked, "but it's 1000 HP." I flashed her my best lady-killer-smile before I forgot I didn't have a lady-killer smile. I'd never been one to flirt. This was painful! Why didn't they teach this stuff in school? I'd do boot camp a hundred times if it meant I never had to flirt.

I approached my truck and opened her door like a perfect escort. I was clearly racking up bonus points with all my gentlemanly ways. It was too bad I had to compete with that stupid king. I set the basket in the box and then ran around to my door, jumped in, and cranked the engine. I took off toward the castle.

I thought she would remain quiet, but she initiated small talk. "Thanks for the ride. I'm sorry if I interrupted your plans in town."

"Oh no," I assured her. "I was only there to get a pipe fitting to fix a leaky pipe, but it was so busy, I was on my way out."

"Do you have plumbing problems?" Her brow lowered as if she actually cared about plumbing systems.

"It's been an ongoing issue." I drummed my fingers on my steering wheel, as I diagnosed while I spoke, "Since the place sat empty for so long, I'm beginning to suspect there's something bigger going on. I'll switch out this fitting for now, and see if I get water again. If not, I'll have to try something else."

"Ah, you have no water?" Her chin inclined to a thoughtful angle. "What are you doing for cooking and showers?"

"Well." I slowed the truck, taking the bend in the road that led to the castle hill. "I've been grabbing water from town—"

"But you didn't get any today because of me," she cut me off, empathy hinting in her tone.

"Not because of you—" I tried to tell her the rest of the sentence. The part that said this was better. I'd rather thirst for days than miss this opportunity to see her one more time, but she gave me one of those smiles I was beginning to memorize. It was higher on one side, and should come with a black box warning because it had the force to stop my heart.

She pointed out her window. "You might want to slow up here, because of the guards. I'll have to explain what's happening, but hopefully Weston's at his post."

My truck crawled forward, my heart ticking up when I spotted the infantry soldiers in their uniforms. I tightened my grip on the steering wheel so much my knuckles bleached. It wasn't that I missed being a soldier because I didn't. However, the uniforms sent my mind back to a place that stole the air from my lungs.

I turned into their long driveway, my truck jostling forward, finding every pothole. It was a very bouncy reminder of all the ways the war was bleeding this country of resources as we hadn't had proper road construction in two years. I winced when I nearly hit my head.

"Ah, Weston's not here." Her smile died as she murmured, "I thought it was odd I could leave the castle without him, but now it makes sense. He must be on his day off."

"What does that mean?"

"Weston's my personal guard, but he's more than that. He's a friend and he never narcs on me. I was hoping he'd cover for me." She rolled down her window and waved toward the guards. "Are you kidding me?" She moaned. Her face blanching.

"What's wrong?" I leaned forward, trying to see where her gaze was fixed.

"Father's standing out front. He never comes out for air. What is he doing?" Sticking her head out the window, she called toward the king, "I'm getting a ride home from a friend."

Neither the king, nor the soldiers, twitched as they stood in line, and we passed with ease. "Is it weird living with soldiers around you all of the time?" I asked with the feeling of a light trance with the uniforms still in view.

"I don't think it's as weird as being a soldier."

Suddenly the back of my throat burned. It hadn't dawned on me before that she might actually know something about me. "How did you know I was a soldier?"

"I asked father about you after you yelled at me for being on your land. He confirmed he had sold his land to a soldier." She motioned to the driveway that split off from the main circular drive. "You can park up here."

I swallowed, hating that people talked about me. "It's not weird anymore since it's over." I tried not to mutter.

The king waved with an inviting smile on his face. "Mr. Mathews, I thought that was you." He strode over to the truck and peered inside. "I should have known Erralee was off napping again. She's been sleeping in that field since she was knee-high. I should have warned you when I sold you the land."

"It's fine." My lips curled into a genuine grin. "I'm getting quite used to her."

Her dad motioned toward the parking garage. "Since you are here, you might as well pull in, and stay for dinner tonight."

"Nah, I got work—" My auto-anti-people nature kicked in before I could see what was happening. I had been invited to eat with the king—*the exact person I needed to talk to!* I interrupted my own words, "Well, I wouldn't want to be any trouble."

"For being a guest?" His brows raised. "No trouble at all. You're our neighbor, and a friend."

I bit back a victory smile as this was too perfect! Once I explained to him how the farmstead he sold me was absolute junk, and I still didn't have running water, he'd have to consider selling me the bigger farmstead across the highway. "If you insist."

"I do."

I didn't want to appear too eager, so I downplayed my excitement, "I would be honored to stay, but I hope I'm not underdressed."

"Oh," His eyes grazed my ranch wear. "There's probably time for you to shower. My butler can find you something proper to wear."

"If it's okay with Erralee." I looked back at her, as she had been quiet the entire conversation, sitting unmoving on the bench seat next to me.

She was biting the corner of her lip, looking intrigued, and quickly added, "Certainly. It would be a pleasure for you to stay."

"It's settled." Erralee's father pointed forward, ushering me to a parking spot as I drove up. As I parked the truck, I caught Erralee's eyes. "I didn't expect a dinner invitation. I hope it's okay. I didn't want to be rude by turning your father down."

"It's perfectly fine," she quipped. "I'm glad you're here. In a way, it feels as if I have someone on my side." She opened the door and jumped down before I had a chance to assist her. "Come on, I'll introduce you to Father's butler." She slammed the truck door, leading me toward the castle.

I was doing ninja kicks in my head. Completely clueless about how this opportunity to dine with the king fell into my lap, but it had to be fate. Part of me wanted to slow down and take in the environment. I'd never been to the castle before. It looked better than in the pictures, but I didn't have time to stare because Erralee was hurrying, and I struggled to keep up with her. "You are so different from what you'd imagine from a princess." My words floated out a little softer than expected, but I was in awe of how she actually lived here.

She guffawed, tossing her head back slightly, before spitting out, "That's probably why Father was so quick to trade me away."

"Don't say that," I continued in a lower tone. "I don't think that's how it went at all. King Aswell saw how special you were."

"Either way, it's a done deal." Her voice was so remorseful, a reply would have been disrespectful.

We passed through the front door, and my eyes quickly floated to the cathedral-high ceilings and crystal chandeliers that were bigger than my truck. Adrenaline trickled through my veins, happily feeding me with a surge of energy, and I held my breath. *Don't screw this up . . .*

Ten

Princess Erralee

Something at the castle was off and getting harder to ignore. This morning I had assumed the castle was quiet because of Father's meetings with King Aswell. Now I realized the stillness was because of Weston's absence. It was unusual for a midweek day. He hadn't told me he was going to be gone, so he must have gotten sick.

In an odd way his absence was perfect timing because it gave me the freedom to do what I wanted—even more than when I'm on his watch. As I led Reeves through the hall, I did my best to hide my attraction to him. It was silly, really. I was getting engaged tonight. I certainly didn't need to feel as if my heart could beat out of my chest just being near him. I blamed it on the basket of roses. It was bittersweet, though, because it's not like anything could happen between us. I had been honest about my situation, and we were from two completely different worlds.

"Okay." I motioned to the guest suite where Father's butler was waiting. "Davis is here, and he's the best. Just do what he says, and I'll meet you downstairs." I continued to my room where Margarette was just stepping out.

"I laid out your gown in your dressing room," she simply stated as if something was unusual about tonight. Usually, she stayed and waited for me to dress and assist with my hair. Not tonight.

"Thank you." I glanced at my bed, finding the red satin dress I had gotten last Christmas. Never in a million years would I select that one for tonight. It was too formal, not to mention more of a ball gown. With this war raging on forever, I didn't feel as if I could celebrate anything. Not even my engagement tonight. I'd feel best in black. "Is there a reason you need to leave?" I called over my shoulder, hoping to catch her before she went downstairs. The red dress told me she understood tonight was special. Why wouldn't she help me with my hair?

She stopped on her heel, and took a couple of steps back, speaking quietly, "I had my hours cut. I volunteered time tonight because this dinner is important. I got every-thing set out for you." She tugged on her lips, pulling them into an obviously forced smile. "Perhaps Ruenella can as-sist you." She motioned down the hall toward Ruenella's suite. "Why don't I check with her before I leave?"

"Sure." I hesitated in the hall, watching her leave then I eyed my red dress from the doorway. My world was splitting in two. Everywhere around me people were asked to make sacrifices. I didn't doubt Margarette's hours were cut to save money, which was not fair. She has worked here since I was a baby. Reeves even lost his hand for this stupid war. Here I am scowling at a red dress. Was it really that much to sacrifice for what I'd gain? My friends and family could go back to a normal life. Where'd they feel safe again. I don't even remember the last time I could breathe normally without this stupid lump in my throat. Everything was changing so fast.

I sighed, not heavily. It was quiet. Serene. Maybe I was finally getting used to this idea? I went inside and dutifully got ready. When a knock sounded on my door, I hoped it was Margarette to inspect me. Instead, Ruenella plowed through the door with a ginormous smile.

"You!" she called in a teasing tone. "You did not just bring a date to dinner. Father is going to lose himself."

"He's not my date," I assured her, trying my best to sound bored with this as I fluffed my hair. "He's the neighbor who gave me a ride home. Father already knows because he's the one who invited him. Not me."

Ruenella's smile pulled so wide she squealed. "Are you blind?" she gushed. "He is so good looking. You are sure to make King Aswell jealous."

I tugged the brush through my hair, cringing through the tangles. "I'm not trying to make anyone jealous. Again, Father invited him, and I honestly didn't think that much about it. Remember, I'm getting engaged tonight."

"You should have thought about it. Things are getting interesting. Father is downstairs asking Reeves war strategies questions."

"Wait!" I turned to her, my jaw almost hitting the floor. "Reeves is already downstairs with Father?"

"Yeah, that's where I saw him—"

"Oh boy," I murmured. They didn't need to be kept separate. I had only assumed I would be in the room when they talked. Father put on a strong front, but his mental health was much too fragile to risk any direct questions about the war. Reeves was a vet, but I didn't know his opinion about that stuff, and I'd assumed since he lost a hand and all, it might not be the most favorable. I set my brush down on my vanity. My hand hovered over my tube of lipstick. Mother always insisted I looked better with the finishing touch of lipstick. Not the red one, that made me look cheap. Her words, not mine. It was totally messed up, and as if all my nerves were bundling over with everything I'd been through this week, my fingers trembled above the tube of lipstick, refusing to touch it.

It had somehow become a symbol of everything they forced me to change. I'd never be perfect enough for my family.

I checked over my shoulder. Ruenella was already headed toward the door with her back toward me. With one swift motion, I bumped the tube, and it rolled forward over the edge of the vanity, getting lost between the wall and the piece of furniture. Then I spun on my heel, heading for Father's study. "I'd better get down there before things get out of hand."

I scurried down the hall, slipping my shoes on as I went since I wasn't allowed to be barefoot when we had guests. It was another one of the dumb royal etiquette rules. It seemed petty, but it was my least favorite rule. I can understand not chewing with your mouth open, or waiting your turn to speak, but having to wear high heels when you're in your own home is absurd.

I slowed as best as I could, trying to quiet the click of my heels on the marble floor. Father, King Aswell, and Reeves were all seated in a circle on the leather chairs in Father's study like they were part of some boy's club. Thankfully, they didn't hear me approach, and I listened from the door unashamedly, trying to go unnoticed.

"It's not just about the air support," I overheard Reeves say, his entire demeanor and appearance altered. Davis had dressed him in a navy suit, the perfect color to saturate the spark in his eyes. He was all the way across the room, but I could tell his eyes were blue from here. I tried ignoring the pitter patter in my chest that should not happen. "All your air support is doing is dropping bombs. You need more ground troops and more medics," he continued. "I laid out in the field for two days waiting for rescue. I would not have lost my comrade if you'd had your men supported."

My hand flew to my chest. I did not think Reeves would do this! He's laying into Father, expecting him to take accountability. Father does not take accountability! Not in public anyway. This was only going to add more stress to him. He knows he is failing. He certainly did not need guilt laid on him now. I loudly cleared my throat, announcing my position, and waited for their eyes to shift. They all stood, instantly silencing.

"I see you didn't waste time getting to know each other." I slid one foot in front of the other into the room, trying to sound casual. My eyes paced the room as I wasn't sure where I should stand. King Aswell and I were getting engaged, but it did not feel natural to stand by him. I was most comfortable near Reeves, but that would have been inappropriate. As much as I despised Father, I stopped nearest him.

"Why, yes," Father's voice was loud, as if he was proclaiming pride, but he couldn't hide the tremble from me, revealing the tension. "I will always remember Reeves for his brave service. Now he's our neighbor. I'm very humbled to have him for dinner."

My gaze bounced to King Aswell, expecting to see a confused, or perhaps worried expression. He was stoic. He appeared to be the kind of man who had bold confidence and didn't get jealous. Not that he had anything to be jealous about . . .

Reeves pinned on a crooked smile as he beamed back at me. I bet it was a surreal moment for him. Father tried hard to be mostly approachable with the townspeople to keep his rating. Still, he didn't make it a habit to dine with them. Not at the castle anyway. Of course, Reeves being a veteran gave him an elevated status.

"Let's not bore the princess with our talks of war." Father gestured forward. "We can go through to the dining room now."

I led the way, not sure who I was supposed to sit by, but Father announced Reeves was getting the head of the table opposite of him, which put Reeves next to Ruenella. There was only one chair left, right between Reeves and King Aswell. I lowered myself, not sure where I was supposed to fix my gaze. How did I get into this mess?

Contrary to the recent modest meals of soup, or poultry from one of our farms, tonight's meal was a feast set to impress. The finest china, the heirloom set with gold overlay that my grandmother had been gifted from a foreign emperor on her wedding, was set out. Long white candlesticks in gold holders lined the middle of the table. Huge platters of shrimp, and roasted lamb with fresh rosemary sprigs as garnish sat in the center. It had been months since we had dined like this, and even though everything looked amazing, I somehow lost my appetite even more.

As soon as I set my linen napkin on my lap, I could feel someone's heated gaze on me. I didn't have to look to know it was Father. We hadn't spoken about my plans tonight, but I was sure Mother had told him. It was obvious all the fuss with the dress and the feast had been planned to be a celebratory one for my engagement.

Funny how my heart could feel so heavy on the eve of what should be such a joyous event. My gaze floated to King Aswell. Once again, he was impeccably dressed, in a long black velvet coat, with red piping. I could see how women would find him attractive, especially since he took such care of his looks. Although I found his hook nose slightly less jarring now and had mostly gotten used to seeing him, I felt nothing when I looked at him.

Okay, that was a lie.

I felt dread.

I wished more than anything that I could force myself to feel something positive. Even curiosity, or friendship, would be better than this. It would make everything much easier, but it was not there. Not even a spark. I can't recall one laugh we shared or even a genuine smile I had in his presence. I didn't think I was asking for too much to want to marry someone who made me look forward to our life. Someone who I loved more than anything. Someone who loves me for . . . me. Tears budded in the back of my eyes when my mind recalled Reeves practically begging me to wait to get married. Those were his words. I agreed with him then. I agreed with him even more now. I wanted to marry someone who loved *me*, not my royal position, but I was out of time.

"Tell me, Reeves," Father's commanding voice broke my thoughts. "How is the farmstead coming along?"

Reeves sat tall, as if he'd been waiting days to give a report to my dad. Something about it was endearing. It was clear he was thrilled with his land, and nobody had to ask me how I felt about those fields. They were the prettiest in the entire kingdom. Now that I knew I was leaving, I was grateful they had been sold to Reeves. They were too special for Father. They deserved someone who would love them as I did.

"It's been an honor to step into this landscape and pick up traditions." Reeves paused and cleared his throat, looking rather nervous. "I appreciate very much that you selected me to be the one to have this privilege."

Father stabbed a piece of his lamb and held it on his fork as if it helped to make his point. "That piece of land is the best of the best. I'm sure Erralee will miss it." He popped the meat into his mouth and chewed while peering at me. I involuntarily coughed, feeling something stuck in my throat even though I hadn't eaten anything. It clearly was the lump of betrayal Father just lodged deeper in there. I never assumed it had been an accident he sold my favorite field. It hadn't dawned on me until now, that perhaps he could have asked me about how I felt first. He didn't care about my opinion. Had he known all along when he sold that field that I was next? Covering my throat with my hand, I swallowed, mustering up saliva to move the lump. When that didn't work, I grabbed my glass of water, and took several large gulps.

Reeves side-eyed me, as he appeared to be the only one at the table to notice I was visibly struggling. As I set down my nearly empty glass, Reeves replied to Father, "It was a surprise the first couple of days to find a princess napping in my field." His eyes hovered over me, pinning me in place. My heart beat as if it were going to knock down the walls of my chest. That was all before he tacked on, "She might be the best part."

"What's this I hear?" King Aswell cut in, his eyes locking on me with a murky smile. "Do you sleep outside?"

It wasn't a big deal. I wasn't embarrassed. Anyone who knew me understood that's what I did, but the warning glare I got from Father told me to downplay it. "Um, well, when it's nice out. Like on summer days, I enjoy the sun. Sometimes I have accidentally fallen asleep . . ."

"Interesting." King Aswell's tone was curt. Not rude, but something about it made me feel juvenile. I don't know what hobbies he expected me to have, but I couldn't help but like what I liked. I lowered my gaze to my plate and pushed my lamb around with my fork. Even though this was the most impressive meal we'd had in months, I was now thoroughly disgusted with the food.

King Aswell's presence cast a shadow on my mood. For a man trying to marry me, he sure didn't make any effort to lift me up, or banter. It's like he thought he didn't need to court me or impress me. I supposed he can have that attitude since he's a king, but I was saddened. I wanted the kind of love that was in fairytales. The one people spoke about that made their hearts race. I seriously struggled to make eye contact with this man.

"I can't blame her," Reeves politely interjected. "It's one of the most beautiful spots. She has excellent taste." Reeves was smiling ear to ear. I'm sure he was smitten to be having dinner at the castle. I was happy he was here. After everything he'd been through for this country, he deserved a nice meal. It was oddly striking how he'd been through all this suffering on the actual front lines of war, and he wore the biggest smile in a room full of royals.

Well, maybe not the biggest. Ruenella was beaming brighter than a July sun as she batted her lashes at Reeves. She didn't have a single renegade hair. She must have spent all afternoon preparing for this dinner. She always was more into the pomp and pageantry than I was. Eager to get eyes off of me, I brought her into the conversation. "Ruenella, how was your day?"

"It was lovely." Her rouged cheeks turned ever pinker. "My trainer was here this morning for Pilates. Then I had brunch in my room while I curled up in bed with a book, and it was so captivating, I had to read the whole thing."

"Is that so?" King Aswell's head tilted, his eyes latching on Ruenella. "Anything we need to know about?"

"Unless you like historical romance." She raised both shoulders into a polite shrug. "I'm guessing you'd pass."

Father cleared his throat, directing his gaze back on Reeves. "What crops are you planning for next spring?"

"I'm going to do the usuals: wheat, sugar beets, and potatoes." His eyes moved over mine. "I had planned on planting sunflowers in Erralee's field, but that was before I found out what a great nap spot that was. I might have to leave it for her."

"Interesting," Father mused as he wiped his mouth with his napkin. We all waited while he finished swallowing and set his napkin in his lap to hear the rest of this thought. "We've never had sunflowers on any of our farms. I'd be curious to see how they fare."

"I'll let you know," Reeves replied with his gaze on Father. He was stirring his food with his fork in a random pattern. He obviously did not even know he was doing it as it appeared to be a nervous fidget. He managed to push off most of his vegetables onto the heirloom tablecloth. I covered my mouth, suppressing a giggle.

I'd spent so many dinners with all the most impressive people who had perfect table manners. Never had I witnessed something so improper in front of my father. Yet, it was so endearing, and refreshing to see someone who was not fake. Reeves was himself. A real person, just being who he was. I only gained more respect for him when he further explained his goals to Father, "To be honest," he said. "I'd love to add safflowers. I'd like to eventually acquire the field on the other side of the road for those." He tilted his head toward Father. "Just to throw that out there . . . if you're ever interested in *selling* that land, I have a plan for it."

"And tell me this." Father smacked his lips as he shoveled more duck into his mouth. He'd cleared so much meat on that plate, you'd think he hadn't eaten in months. "What's special about that field?"

"Erralee's field has shadows in the evening from the large buttes." He paused, clearing his throat, as he adjusted his posture to get even taller. "They are lovely, but it does not make for the best sun, except in the morning . . . while Erralee naps." He shot me a teasing grin, but quickly replanted his focus back on Father. "Safflowers need harvesting in full sun, or they get sticky, and you risk plugging up your machinery. I can imagine the harvest of them in Erralee's field would take days as we'd only have an hour or two each morning." Reeves chuckled in a reminiscent manner. "I've learned the hard way not to risk it. But the north fields are full sun and hold water well."

I zoned out on the farm stuff, as I focused on watching Father's lips tighten while he listened. I could not read him well, but he appeared to be soaking up Reeves' plans. However, he remained silent on what his plans were for that plot of land or even the rest of his farms, which frankly left me unsettled. *Would we even have food to eat?* I had been unaware, until recently how badly we were bleeding resources, because Father had hidden it. I wasn't a political type, but I wondered what happened when an entire dynasty went bankrupt. I honestly had no clue. Would another country control us? The thoughts added to the budding pressure I already held in my chest. I spent the rest of the meal not comprehending a word as I tried to pep talk myself into thinking everything would be okay.

I had the power to fix this before we lost everything.

The sudden clanging of dishes brought me back to reality. Servants had returned to the room, clearing our plates. Everyone but Mother had stood up, loitering near the table with drinks in their hands. They were obviously headed to the Grand Hall. Mother was intently staring at me. I checked my dress to ensure it hadn't gotten spilled on. The dress was in perfect condition without even one wrinkle. I lowered my brow, and whispered, "What is it?"

Her forehead scrunched in an unbecoming way before she leaned in close. "I thought you had decided last night. Everyone has been walking on eggshells all day to see if you follow through. I find it *ridiculous* you have kept King Aswell waiting like this. What could possibly be more important than this!"

My eye twitched, as if begging me to turbo blink in disbelief. I never asked for a leadership role in this family, and the weight of pressure was becoming unbearable. All I wanted was to believe that I was entering into a marriage where I would be loved. I hadn't received any such hint that this marriage was anything more than a peace treaty. Was it too much to want to wait for my own true love? I guess it is when you are me ... I gritted my teeth and spoke through them. "I intend to follow through, Mother. I spent the day saying goodbye to friends in town. I didn't know what I'd be forced into once I entered this engagement." Even though it was against my nature, I added in a sarcastic tone. "Forgive me for needing *one day* to live my life."

"I don't need to remind you that King Aswell is not a fool," she hissed. "If anything, you are his charity case. He's doing us a great favor, and please don't ruin this."

My face blanched, and my insides iced over. Mother had never spoken to me like this before. The desperation in her voice distressed me. I scooted my chair back in one swift push and stood as I steeled my jaw. "I'll take care of it tonight." Then I turned on my heel and left, tears budding in my eyes.

As I scurried off, I pretended not to hear Mother's instructions for me. "Do freshen up. And put some lipstick on ..."

Eleven

Reeves

Heading toward the castle exit, I was amazed at how tonight had gone. I had gotten so much time to talk to the King, and I think I'd impressed him. He didn't say he would sell me the land, but some of the other stuff he said intrigued me. He had spoken about hiring a central farming manager to coordinate rotations between his farms. The questions he asked seemed like a job interview. *Would I be interested in something like that?* I wasn't sure, but then again, it would put me further in line for acquiring more land and getting in even better favor.

There was nothing wrong with that.

Davis, the butler, handed me my bundle of work clothes, while gesturing to the clothes I had been lent. "Just keep the suit." He escorted me to the foyer, but when we rounded the corner, I got a glimpse of Erralee, who also appeared to be on her way out.

Both her feathered brows sprang high when she saw us. "I was, ah, going to get some air." She had huge tears running down her cheeks, but she quickly slapped them away when she saw us. All the triumph I had over my evening instantly dissipated with the sadness etched into Erralee's face.

"It's dark out, my lady," the butler reminded her with an air of suspicion in his voice.

"Perhaps, I can have a minute of your time." I stepped forward, my heart pounding out a rhythm that only comes when it's filled with adrenaline. Time was running out . . . Erralee had expressed to me how upset she was about this marriage, but tonight I got to witness it. It wasn't right. You don't win wars with unjust marriages. My heart wrenched so strongly for her, I struggled to speak. "This is probably a final goodbye."

"Sure." Her eyes snapped to the butler, and she mumbled, "I'll just be outside." She swung open the door as if busting out of jail and I followed her. As soon as the door was shut, she let out a sigh like she was painfully falling, before bursting into tears.

I didn't need to ask her what was wrong, because I had seen the whole night play out. To say she wasn't matched well with King Aswell was a massive understatement. The little she tried to engage him, he seemed to almost belittle her. She appeared repulsed by him, and he did nothing to soothe her. I wasn't a Casanova, but it didn't take Romeo to see everything about their arrangement was off.

She had held her head high through dinner, but her family refused to see under her poorly acted façade. Burying her face in her hands, she wept for several beats before finally speaking through broken sobs, "How am I ever going to do this?"

The urge to comfort her took me by surprise. I dared to step closer to her. Pausing an arm's reach away as I was sure someone was watching us. My sunbaked lips parted but I made no sound.

"Reeves," she said through sobs, "do you think this is a bad idea?"

Empathy wrapped my heart. I hiked a brow, but it was the kind of limp expression you give when you try to meet the bare minimum of manners, while still fighting to be honest about your lack of approval. Being in the army, I traveled extensively, meeting many interesting characters. I was rather good at sizing up people. I didn't get bad vibes from King Aswell, but when I looked at Erralec . . . she was so innocent. *Sooo naive.* I mean, the girl's main hobby was nature naps. Even if the guy turned out to be a half decent human being, Erralee clearly wasn't ready for marriage. Definitely not a marriage of oil and water.

Guilt crept into my throat as I thought this over. I had used dinner to my advantage to get what I wanted. Actually, my entire friendship with Erralee had been forged because I was trying to get close to her dad. Now, seeing her so broken, I couldn't care less about getting my land. If I thought it would make her truly happy, I'd give up her old land, too.

There wasn't a clear way to fix this.

I didn't know anything about arranged marriages, but I had my turn with fear. I could speak to that. "I ah, remember the night before I went on my first attack mission," I started, wetting my lips. "I was a pool of sweat, wondering how I ever allowed myself to be duped into putting my life on the line. I kept thinking someone else should have to be the one on the front line." I paused, nervously scratched my head, and rested my hand on my neck as it felt good to just hold on to something. "But then I thought, what kind of life is that? Someone who looks the other way on injustice, yet benefits from the sweat of others. I didn't want to run from my fears."

I dipped my eyebrows at the battlefield memories that flashed. Erralee's eyes brimmed with flecks of gold that glittered amongst the blue-violet of her eyes. In the tiniest voice, as if she was afraid to make a sound, she breathed, "How do I get over the fear?"

"Remember you don't ever get over it. Just when it's the scariest, you face it. And who knows." To make her smile, I pulled one side of my lips into an unconvincing lopsided grin. "Maybe you'll end up having a frolicking good time." *I didn't mean she marries King Aswell. We both know that is not the good time she needs. A fairytale plays in my mind. One where we spend more days climbing on rocks, jumping into lakes, laughing until we tire out to eventually nap in the sun. The images surprise me enough to make my breath grow shallow. I hadn't really thought about that stuff with her before. Now that I did, it's the only thing that would make sense. It made more sense than her marrying King Aswell. I don't tell her that part.*

She shuddered; She actually appeared numb to the cold, but her discomfort started from the conversation. I noticed that once again, her arms were bare. I slipped my jacket off and draped it on her shoulders. "You sure do make a habit out of not grabbing a coat."

"You always have one for me." Her fingers pulling the collar tight around her. "Are you saying I need to hurry and get it over and marry him? Just do my part."

"Woo, that's not what I said, exactly." I scratched my head again, getting a little dizzy at the thought of her marrying this man. My lips parted, pausing as I thought about my hesitation. I wasn't scared about not getting my land anymore. I had spent the last two hours with her dad, and we'd come to friendly terms. I didn't doubt there'd be opportunities for me at some point. I ran my tongue over my lips as I mulled this over, and I realized . . . I was scared for her, but not because she was mismatched. Plenty of people survived marriages of convenience and learned to thrive. Maybe they would? In movies it always worked out.

Something was happening as I stared at her.

A synchronizing.

My initial intentions to get close to her had been one hundred percent selfish, and for better access to her father. Somewhere along the way . . . that changed. When I looked at her, I knew what she was feeling.

Correction. I felt what she was feeling.

Part of me said to confess my ill intentions. The other half said I should tell her I was starting to have feelings for her. The other half, because I'm overly complicated and have more halves than the average person said, *just hold her.*

And that's the half I listened to.

I barely extended my arms, and she flew right into them, unleashing a new wave of sobs right onto my shoulder. I didn't have words to describe what was happening. Somehow, we'd both broken through each other's bravado. What was left was raw.

I couldn't tell her she'd be okay if she got married, because a part of me was now angry with her. It truly was unfair, and I selfishly wondered what would have happened if *we* had been allowed to continue our organic friendship. Sure, princesses didn't date cowboys, but Erralee was far from an ordinary princess.

I wanted to scream at her not to do it. Give her another option and tell her we could have a life together. *Possibly?* But as I was standing here holding her, Elliot's face floated in my mind. He gave up his life for this country, and so many more of the men I fought with. I couldn't tell her not to do it. I'd honestly witnessed braver things. She was in the position to change history and be an international hero. I couldn't take that from her. My heart was splitting in two, completely torn, neither choice had a happy ending. I can't imagine how she was feeling if I felt this heartache.

She sobbed into my shoulder, and let my fingers caress her long strands of hair until she was out of tears. What I did manage to say when she finally lifted her face was, "Whatever you decide, you have an amazing destiny to fulfill, and I'll be cheering you on from the sidelines."

She blinked in rapid succession, but before she could say anything, the door opened again, and the butler stood intrusively close to us. Her gaze floated to him, and then back to me, and she squeaked out, "I'd better go in."

My feet cemented until the door banged closed behind her, a piece of my heart crumbled in the echoes of the slam.

Twelve
Princess Erralee

Thankfully, Father was in his study with the door closed. Cigar smoke wafted from under the door, and I'm sure he was deep in his glass of scotch and his staring contest with his fireplace flames. I didn't dare make a sound as I tiptoed past the door. Seeing him again tonight would make this much worse. I swiped away my tears and went looking for King Aswell.

It was time to follow through.

I understood we were in an era of war, and I could never pursue selfish desires. I was here to serve a higher purpose. I now see how Reeves was put into my life to show me that. He selflessly fought in this war, giving a limb for his country, not even knowing if he'd live. I can move to another castle. It would mean I'd have to deny these budding feelings for Reeves . . . but we were always an impossibility anyway.

It was time for my mission to begin.

I found King Aswell exactly where I had predicted in the library, with an open book on his lap and a tablet glowing by his side, opened to a news website. I stood in the doorway watching him for a long moment. His long face was shadowed from looking down. Would I ever be able to look at him with anything more than a cringe? I didn't want my heart to be this hardened. Maybe under different circumstances, that hadn't felt so out of control, I would have felt more comfortable, but everything about this agreement was wrong.

My chin quivered, and I grasped the door frame, steadying myself. There was no turning back now. Had I been brave enough earlier, I could have avoided the recent war surge. Everything felt as if it were riding on me. Swallowing the last of my selfish dreams, I stepped forward into the room.

Just as he turned the page of his book, his gaze shifted. Immediately he rose to his feet. "Erralee, what a nice surprise." When I didn't say anything, because I was too busy choking on my tears, the corners of his mouth bent, and he took a step forward. "What's wrong?"

I shook my head, letting my gaze float up in total avoidance as I blinked back the sting in my eyes. *I'm such a* fool. I'm a princess in a castle with everything I could ever want. I fought back spoiled tears. Tears that said I didn't want to help my people live. It was really that simple. I had a chance to save lives. *It wasn't about me.* Placing a hand on my chest, my throat heated as if it was preparing for the lies. "I heard about the ambush."

"Yes. It's getting close to home." His chin raised thoughtfully into a melancholy expression. "Your father and I have been studying strategies." The lines on his forehead caved deeper, but they didn't look unattractive. Just weary. Suddenly, I understood him and why he was the way he was, with his books and his serious ways. He was smart. A leader who had built one of the strongest armies, and he was prepared to help my father. He was the kind of man history books were filled with.

I bit my lip, ready to speak, but my mouth wouldn't open. Every nerve in my body stood in alarm, screaming at me that something was off. This offer was too good to be true, and it wasn't my path.

"You're shaking," King Aswell said after I failed to say anything. His chin dipped sympathetically.

"I'm scared."

He stepped forward, erasing most of the space between us. Lowering his gaze, he trapped my eyes and a spiral of fear ripped through my body. "You don't have to be afraid." Opening his hand, he reached out to me.

My feet froze to the floor, which was the best thing that could have happened, because they stopped me from fleeing. I had finally run out of fighting spirit. "And if I don't love you right away—" My voice dropped off because the air from my chest gave out. I wasn't prepared to feel I was dying when I was trying to save lives.

His eyes held mine, and in the soft glow of the library, they were warm and kind. I held onto that as the hope that someday, I might remember this moment and laugh at how silly I had been. *I am marrying a king, after all. It had to work out . . .*

"One day at a time," he whispered.

I swallowed again, but the knot didn't budge. It made taking a deep breath impossible, and I was getting light-headed. He reached his hand out further, brushing his finger with mine. I held my breath as I slipped my hand in his. He brought it to his lips and placed a kiss on each of my fingers. His lips felt dry and scratched my fingertips, but I didn't stiffen. Instead, I felt a tiny bit of relief as I was now finally confident this war could be won.

We would have peace.

That's the only thing that mattered.

He let my hand go, and he smiled at me warmly. "Can you call me Jon?"

"Jon," I echoed, barely getting the word over the knot in my throat. It definitely didn't roll out smoothly and stuck in my heart like a giant hardened spitball. I took one more swallow. This time it was more of a gulp that finally broke past the lump. I was mostly numb by now, enough so I could speak about my fate. "I will marry you, Jon."

His eyes moistened in the corners in a way that surprised me. "I promise to do everything I can to make you the happiest woman in the world. *Our* country will be proud to have you as Queen."

I believed he spoke the truth, but I felt nothing but impending doom.

My path was marked.

"It's late in the evening," I squeaked out. "If it's okay, I'd rather we chat more in the morning when I'm fresh."

"Of course." He dipped his head, bringing his lips down and pressed a chaste kiss to the crown of my head. "Goodnight."

I forced a tight-lipped smile, feeling awkward that I couldn't be more affectionate, and spun on my heel. I prayed he didn't catch the glisten of tears in the corners of my eyes as I hurried back to my room where I cried most of the night.

When I got up the next day, I was feeling surprisingly calm. Maybe I'd cried all my tears? I sure didn't get any sleep, but it was as if a security blanket had wrapped me tightly, taming my fears. The war was going to end. I could start my day with a clear head.

I slipped into a beige dress. One with flowy bell sleeves that cinched into a high waist. Beige felt safe for today. It wasn't an overly optimistic color, but it was not grieving like black. Just beige. It fit my mood perfectly.

As I descended the stairs on my way to breakfast, the scent of bacon grease met my nose, making my stomach rumble. I never ate a bite for dinner last night, and my appetite was piqued. It had been a long time since my father had a hog butchered. He was obviously celebrating. This was a good thing, me getting married. Positive things could happen now. My hand glided over the smooth railing as I quickened my descent down the grand staircase. I was ready for things to get better.

The memory of Jon kissing my head last night pulled to the front of my mind. It was a simple gesture, but the sweetness wasn't lost. I understood how awkward this had to be for him. Perhaps, I'd been too hard on him?

As I passed by the front room, I peeked out the window and noticed that, once again, Weston was not at his post. He rarely took a vacation, but when he did, someone else was dutifully assigned to my watch. Nobody had said any-thing.

Has Father fired him to save money? He cut Margarette's hours . . .

Shaking my head, I pushed the thought out of my mind, though there remained a niggling in the back of my brain. It would make sense when I left the palace, Weston's job wouldn't be needed since he was my personal guard. *Will Father let him go?* That would be awful for him, because he helped to provide for his single mother and little sister.

Father would never do that.

But a week ago, I would never have thought my father would sell my field, or force me into a marriage. Getting rid of my guard was logical at this point, especially since something wasn't adding up.

For the last three days, I'd been parading around without any security, and no one had said anything . . . Why would that be unless they were trying not to draw attention to his absence? A cold wave of fear washed over me, and suddenly it all made sense. *Father let Weston go.* Anger bubbled in my stomach. I was one of the few people who really understood how much he needed his job. Plus, he had been the most loyal friend I'd ever had.

How dare Father do this!

Forgetting all my ladylike manners, I stormed through the hall to Father's study, making as much noise as possible. I found the door open, and he was inside, alone. I charged to the center of the room, planted my feet, and steeled my gaze on his. "Father, where is Weston?"

He didn't flinch, or even raise his gaze. He simply scrolled up on his tablet as he read the morning news. "Why do you ask?"

"You know why I ask." I narrowed my gaze, chewing on my lip as I studied him. His lack of rebuttal confirmed what I had presumed. "You laid him off because I'm leaving the palace. You are trying to save money at his expense, aren't you?"

"No." He raised his gaze to me, parting his lips, but I wouldn't let him speak.

"Don't cover it up," I bit out. "I've never been allowed anywhere without a guard, and for the past three days, nobody has said boo about me running all over without one. Considering we've never had higher security alerts, something is wrong. What is going on?" Sharply parking my hand on my hip, I was ready for answers. I'd never spoken to my father this way, but I had reached my limit.

"He didn't want you to worry." Father crossed his hands in front of him, leaning forward, which was out of character for him.

"Worry about where he will get his next meal from, since you laid him off?" I spit back haughtily.

"Honey," Father's voice lowered, so much so, I had to watch his lips to make out the words. "Weston volunteered to fight on the frontline."

A sarcastic laugh stumbled in my throat. He was joking. He had to be. Weston wasn't a fighter. Father didn't laugh. He didn't even crack a dimple. Suddenly, I felt as if I had been thrown into a brick wall. I reached for the nearest chair, stumbling forward. Images of sweet Weston fighting flashed in my mind. Instantly nauseous and heartsick, I fell on my knees before I made it to the chair. I wailed as if I had been stabbed in the chest. "Why!"

Father pushed back his chair, rounded the desk, and got on a knee. Placing one hand on my back, he held it firmly in silence. I couldn't stomach his muteness.

His silence was a lie!

He didn't have to tell me the frontline was running on barebones. I didn't need to hear it; frankly I couldn't stomach it.

"He had wanted to volunteer for a while, but he couldn't leave you. Since he knew you'd be taken care of by King Aswell, he felt it was his duty."

"You're a liar," I growled through gritted teeth from my place on the floor. "You promised me this war would *end* if I agreed to this marriage. You didn't have to let Weston go. King Aswell had backup." My breath was failing. I struggled to push out the following words, taking long breaths between each one, "You did this to me as punishment."

Father's eyes were dark and unflinching. "He asked to go."

"You're the king. He is your soldier. You own him." My voice was down to a whisper, barely making an appearance at all. I had to speak my peace, or I knew I'd regret it. Someone had to stand up to Father. "Last night, I pledged my future to a man I can't stand so this country can prosper, and you lied to me."

"He asked to go," Father echoed with a piercing stare.

I bit back words that I would regret, and clambered to my feet. I didn't want him to suspect anything, but in my silence, I vowed to be done with this dynasty. I would *not* be loyal to Father. I scampered down the hall, tripping over my own feet. My world blurred, as the tears slid down my face, and though tears can sometimes trickle, these tears were heavy and hot. The burn fueling my legs to run faster.

I didn't have any possessions I cared to pack as I ran down the servants' quarters and out the back. The absence of Weston following me, scolding me to wait up, ripped my heart open. *Will I ever see him again?* Outside, the first snowflakes of an early storm had started to flutter, landing on my already soaked lashes, but I blinked them away. It was a freak snowstorm, a warning that nature was trying to fight back, too. The world could crumble around me at this point and swallow me up, and I wouldn't care.

I paced forward to the men standing on guard.

I already knew the outcome, but found myself frantically searching for Weston.

He wasn't at his post.

He wasn't coming up the driveway.

A giant gap remained between the two guards where he usually stood. It was an odd display of reverence by his fellow soldiers that split the flood gates wide open. How long would there be a gap? Would it always be there?

What if he dies . . .

I balled my hand into a fist and pounded it on my heart. This pain . . . I'd rather die. Father's betrayal. Weston's absence. It all circled my head, and I was so sick of it all. I did my part! It didn't work because they lied!

A rustle of leaves from behind stole my attention.

I held my breath and turned, praying by some miracle it was Weston coming from the shadows and this was some sick joke. *Please be a joke . . .*

No Weston.

It was Ruenella, my beautiful sister. Not a hair out of place, and her makeup was flawless. Her perfectly lipstick-stained lips were pinched as she appeared to be holding her breath, too.

"You knew?" I accused my sister. Not because I didn't love her but because of our loving sisterly bond. My heart rattled in my chest. I felt so betrayed.

Ruenella blew out her breath. "You're in shock." She paused, taking a deep swallow. "Take some time to think about it before you do something irrational. If you leave, Father will disown you, and you'll have nothing."

"I understand that." I held her gaze without flinching. "I understand exactly what I'm losing." I had made up my mind. Father was using everyone as pawns. I barely saw this before it was too late. I wouldn't be one of his pawns.

It'd be easier if I tore off in a fit and didn't think about it until years had passed. Being the younger, more daring sister, I often did things without thinking. And like perfect birth-order rites of passage, Ruenella was always there, forewarning my regrets. "If you leave," Ruenella's jaw quivered as she pressed the issue, "Father will banish you, and anyone who remains in contact with you."

I grabbed her hand and squeezed my fingers between her thin fingers that always felt so much frailer than mine. "Nobody, not even Father, can banish me from you. I'll find a way."

The quiet that comes with heartbreak seeped into our hearts, punctuated by tears in the corner of each of our eyes, as we stood feet cemented to the stone driveway, doing nothing more than staring at each other. Our eyes understood to take in every detail, so our brains would memorize and know what to do with the passage of time. Our hearts understood even the best-case scenario meant it could be *years* before we'd see each other again. Definitely not before the war was over, if there was even a country left by then.

Maybe not even in this lifetime.

"Do you know where you'll go?" Ruenella whispered, also failing to stifle her sobs.

"I don't, but I'll figure it out." I took a few steps away from my dear sister. I couldn't risk getting caught. I needed to move. I also couldn't bear the thought of seeing Mother

disappointed. *Please don't see me run, Mother,* I prayed.
She wouldn't understand, and I wouldn't be able to hold
my tongue. I'd say so many things I would regret.

"I love you," I called over my shoulder as I powered my
legs straight into the forest.

I had no idea where I was going, but it would be far
away, because I couldn't risk getting caught betraying Father. When I neared the edge of the forest, I glanced
back, ready to take in my home for the last time. I loved
my home. An enormous and majestic palace, it towered
over the horizon, with lush spires that nearly reached the
clouds. In the light of day, it drank in the sun's rays, making
all the gardens flourish. It had been a glorious place to grow
up, and a light to the entire kingdom.

My mind turned intrinsically, as I always assumed I was
also a light to the kingdom. Even as a small child, my
presence inspired a reverent silence from any size crowd.
A hush would wash over my entourage, and even the birds
would stop to watch my lilting steps. It was as if I had been
the last crown for a kingdom in ruin, and now I'm getting
banished.

I understood the betrayal I had chosen far too deeply.

I pumped my legs harder, knowing Ruenella would cover
for me, even if it meant her own punishment. Snow was
organically swirling around me now, and I opened my
mouth wide, sucking in all the crisp oxygen to power me
onward.

A part of my heart constricted out an echo, saying, return
home before you have regrets.

The other part turned to stone, declaring it wasn't home anymore.

Regrets are a weakness.
I will not be weak.

Thirteen

Reeves

I grabbed a coffee from the diner and ducked onto the street. Snow fell fast but silent against the earth and was backed by the wind whistling a harsh warning of what was coming. Tucking my chin into the collar of my faded denim jacket, I used my sleeve to brush the fresh film of snow off my windshield before I hopped into the truck and cranked the engine. I sat still for a moment, letting my engine warm.

I'd come to town for groceries, and was glad to have that chore done. With the way this snow was coming down, I didn't have much time to get back home. This snow had come out of nowhere. I'd never seen a fall storm blow like this before. Just a few days ago, Erralee and I were swimming in my creek. I slammed my eyes shut, forcing the memory away. *Forget about her, Reeves. You knew from the beginning she was getting married.*

Needing to fidget to forget about Erralee, *again*, I checked the weather app on my phone. It confirmed what I had suspected. An early winter blizzard was moving in and would bluster for the next three days. Not wanting to risk getting stuck in town, I shifted into gear and headed out. The only reason I stayed on the road was because of the guiding taillights of a semi-trailer in front of me. I entered a complete whiteout as I turned onto the two-lane dirt road to my house. I slowed to barely moving. A single set of car lights passed, their blueish-white glow tinting the snow-white sky, but after that, there was nothing for five miles.

When I turned into my long private drive, I had worked up a sweat on my lower back. Driving in a blizzard was nothing I'd ever learned to be comfortable with. I was relieved to be home. The snow fell at a near-horizontal angle, and the trees were starting to bend under the weight of the snow that had accumulated since last night. The tires of my truck rattled as they bounced off the uneven piles of snow, and out of the corner of my eye—and completely unknown as to how—I spotted someone walking in the ditch.

Who is this idiot trying to catch their death? My house is far from town, and there isn't another residence around for miles. It is way too cold to walk. Dangerous.

Not caring about the ice, I slammed the brakes and immediately pitched my truck into a sideways tailspin. I cranked the wheel and stopped.

I blinked once out of disbelief.

And without a coat.

I rolled down my window. "No naps in the field today." I hollered, trying not to sound like a grump, but she had to be out of her mind. This snow didn't smell like Christmas. It was dangerous and pounding down in ice pellets.

Erralee held her focus forward, her arms wrapped around herself while she trudged through the inches of accumulated snow. At this point, my instincts took over. Here's a woman with all the resources in the world. She wouldn't be out here freezing to death, looking like she was running for her life, unless something was drastically wrong.

I jumped out of my truck, and traipsed behind her, calling, "Will you stop!" I picked up the pace and took a position in front of her, cutting her off. "This is dangerous weather. What's going on?"

Her lips were so pale, they were heathery blue, and didn't have even a quiver left. Expressionless, she stared back at me, as if past the point of going numb. Without waiting for an invitation, I wrapped my arms around her waist and picked her up. She was stiff as a board as I carried her to my truck. I cranked the heater on full blast, took my coat off, and threw it around her shoulders. I tried to hide my concern, but I'd be lying if I didn't say her behavior scared me to death. "I'm not going to ask what you're doing," I said, studying her stoney appearance. "But whatever it is, you'll wait until the storm's over."

She glowered down at her hands, tsking out, "I can't go home."

"I didn't ask you to." I shifted my truck into gear and steered toward the house. Neither one of us muttered a word as we went through the motions of going inside.

I carried in my two bags of groceries in one arm while opening the door for her with the other. She hesitated in my doorway, as if waiting for an invitation. "Come on." I waved her inside. "It's better than outside."

She took a wobbly step forward, and paused, scanning the room. I can't imagine what was going on in her head. Under no other circumstances would I ever invite a member of the royal family into my humble dwelling, especially in the run-down state it's in, but neither of us apparently had better options.

My gaze—ever attuned to my surroundings—caught the black screen above my microwave where the time would ordinarily glow. There was no glow.

The power was out.

Great. I immediately spun on my heel, back toward the door. "It's a good thing I've got plenty of firewood stored in the barn," I muttered to her before jogging outside to the barn, filling my arms to my chin with logs, and hustling back into the cabin. I was breathing heavily as I tossed as many logs as possible to fit into the fireplace. With precision I struck a match on the stone hearth and held it to the fire starter. The fire seeded; I tossed the starter into the logs, and then turned my gaze back to Erralee. She had taken a seat on the couch, slouching all the way down, resting her head back, looking weary.

I ran back to the bedroom, gathered a blanket from my bed, and brought it out and handed it to her. Then I threw a few more logs on the already roaring fire. To say

I was sweating was an understatement, but I didn't feel discomfort.

That'd been numb for years.

By the time I was content with the room's temperature, it was truly a sauna. I turned to check on Erralee, hoping to see some color back in her lips. Better than that, she was sleeping soundly, her cheeks tinting into a warm hue.

It was still rather late in the day for a nap, even for her. Usually, her naps were in the morning when the sun was warm. It was well after lunch time. I grinded my back molars together. Although, she looked rather peaceful now. Something horrible had happened.

Unsettled, I crossed the room, pulling the shabby curtains back and stared out the window. Frost had accumulated along the edges. The window was clearly leaking air, but I could see enough to know the wind was roaring past the house, disturbing everything. It was the thing beyond that wind that felt like the real danger. My nostrils flared. My nerves were usually on edge, but today felt eerie.

I was going find out what was going on.

If I found out that King Aswell—or heaven help me—Erralee's own father had done something to hurt her . . .

They'd better hope this storm buried me alive.

I closed the curtains as best as I could, sealing them in the middle to darken the room for Erralee's rest. I moved near the couch, listening to her breathe.

Keeping watch was something I'd been trained to do.

One thing I was good at, and that's what I did.

Fourteen
Princess Erralee

A brush across my cheek from a rough—but tender—hand, gave me goosebumps, causing my lashes to flutter. My eyes were closed but I could hear the wind moan through the trees outside as they seemed to hum out their own dirge. The air in the room was thick with the scent of burning logs, and ash, potent enough to scratch against my dry throat.

The hand firmly pressed against my forehead, doing some sort of assessment, then softened, lingering for a short moment longer, enough to awaken me more. I opened my eyes.

Reeves.

He was the darkest shape, a mere shadow, sitting alertly with his eyes glued to me. Something about his hushed expression put my mind at ease, and I wasn't afraid.

Mostly confused.

A roaring fire glowed, but other than that, the room was dark. *I was in Reeves' house . . .*

Out of reflex, I pulled myself upright.

Like an avalanche tasked with shattering the peaceful skyline, my memories flooded back. Father sold me.

Weston was at war.

I had run away.

That knot—the one that wrung the bile right from my gallbladder and charged acid into my throat—swelled so tightly, I resisted a dry heave. It was a nightmare. By now Father had to know I was gone. *I never even made it out of the country!* He'd surely be able to find me here. Panic continued to spiral through my chest with each inhale, and my exhale took on more force as I breathed out, "I need to leave."

Reeve's face crept into the soft glow emitted from the fireplace. His lips parted into a neutral position, and heaven-spun blue eyes held a quiet sensitivity, as if he knew all my secrets. "It's one of the worst blizzards in decades." His voice was gruff and sounded as hardened as the stony gaze he held on me. He clearly wasn't going to entertain any pushback from me now. "I found you about ten miles north of my house, on the opposite side of the castle, which means you walked almost twenty miles in a blizzard. You nearly froze to death. You aren't going anywhere."

My voice was weak, my breath barely enough to fill my lungs, let alone support whispering, but I'd been stubborn all my life, and wasn't going to stop now. I pushed my words out, "I, ah, told King Aswell I'd marry him, and I was going to do it." I waited for a beat, sucking more air past my lump. "This morning I found out my father let my guard—Weston, go to the frontlines to fight, and he'd been keeping it a secret."

Reeves' lashes lowered. "I'm sorry."

"I don't even know what that means." I stared forward. My vision was still a little blurry, but slowly adjusting to the dark room. Light haze fogged the room, and I wasn't sure if that was from my dizziness, or the dull ache in my heart. After a moment of introspection, I diagnosed it as the cloud of agony that encapsulated my life.

I squinted, doing my best to make out Reeve's features. He was his usual rugged self, as if he was doing manual labor all day, his blond hair was styled in a buzz cut, almost down to the scalp, clearly not shaking his military habit. He held a take-charge expression, but something else was layered beneath that. An irritation I couldn't place.

When he didn't offer any words, I nervously put him on the spot with a question, "Do you think I overreacted?"

His chin inclined, and he hit me with an indirect gaze as if he were weighing my words for truth. When he still said nothing, I went on the defense. "Weston is my best friend. For Father to send him to the front lines, after he promised to end this war if I married King Aswell . . . I felt like I'd died."

"You don't ever have to explain yourself to me." He shifted, now leaning even closer. His face was so near, it brought his scent of warm musky aftershave, adding to the miasma that already coated the air. The cocktail of scents had a calming effect on me. I hadn't slept more than an hour or two since I had met King Aswell. This entire week had my nervous system in knots. Finally getting away from the castle, even though it wasn't far, had a soothing effect on me and I felt as if my body was purging everything I left behind at the castle. Add to that, the hazy darkened room, and my six hours of traipsing in the snow, terrified out of my mind, I was exhausted. My eyelids wavered from opened to closed.

I searched for Reeves one more time, confirming what I already knew. He was still and sober, right next to me. Everything about this encounter felt like a dream. So much so, my eyes started to drift closed, and before I could resist, I'd fallen back asleep.

I awoke to the sound of someone walking on the roof. Unfortunately, I'd long since left the naivety of my youth to wish for Santa. My eyes grazed the room. It wasn't any different from any of the other farmhouses that father had owned. Each was very modest but had enough space for a family. The living room that I was in had a single plaid sofa in the center, facing a large fireplace with a mounted TV above it. It was clean, without wall hangings on the knotted pine walls and open wood beams that framed an arched ceiling.

The kitchen was adjacent and ran in a L shape along two walls with masculine wood cabinets and darker stone countertops. The entire space was free from clutter. Except for the coat rack by the door, piled with heavy coveralls, and a couple of hats, I could barely tell someone even lived here. It didn't look at all like it used to when the Barnes family lived here.

The Barnes raised three kids, and always kept things piled in every corner. Books or toys. With them being the closest neighbor with kids, Weston and I visited several times in our youth. There was always laughter ringing in the air, and something freshly baked on the stove. Of course, they treated me specially, offering me all the refreshments they had. Often, I wasn't hungry, but I accepted the treats on behalf of Weston. As a growing boy, he always had an insatiable appetite, and I'd stuff the treat in my pocket to give to him later. My gaze dropped to the side as I thought about Weston . . .

Things had changed so much since then. This war was speeding up transformation in the most unpleasant ways. I blinked, pushing the thought of the war away, and rose to my feet, crossing to the window, and listened. Obvious footsteps. Scraping. Then a massive plume of snow tumbled down. *Is he shoveling the roof?*

When his boots dangled down above my head, my suspicion was confirmed. A minute later, he shimmied down, using the porch rail as a step. When he landed on the deck, his eyes caught mine through the window. One side of his lips pulled up into that crooked grin he has, and he immediately pivoted and came inside. "Morning." His voice was softer than expected, as if he was committed to protecting the silence.

"Morning." Surprisingly I wasn't moping. Something about being tucked away at Reeves' house made my whole predicament feel unreal. I obviously couldn't stay here, because I would be found but the storm gave me a respite. "Shoveling the roof?"

Shaking his head, he moved toward the coat hook, removing his boots and heavy coveralls. Snow powdered down on the tiny woven rug beneath him, piling up. "This old house is such a piece of junk; I woke up to water drops in my face. I figured I didn't have long, or I would have a huge mess."

Wrapping my arms across my body, I protected my warmth from the chill the open door had let in. "That's not good."

"I clearly have issues with water." Dropping his hat on the hook next to his coat, he moved to the corner where a little broom was stored and quickly began sweeping the snow back outside, then rushed to close the door. "The pipes, the roof. It's like they are forcing me to move away."

"Let's hope not." It was just a response. It didn't really mean anything, but as soon as the words were out, his head tilted away as if he was trying to hide the tiny smile on his lips.

"I bet you're hungry." Reeves sauntered into the kitchen, removed a pot from the cupboard and looked at me as if wanting an answer. "The power is still out, but I can throw a can of soup in a pot and cook it over the fire."

"Yeah, whatever you have is great." I was self-conscious as I stood back and tried not to feel bad that I couldn't help cook. I didn't want to confess that I had never even made hot water for myself. Maybe I should have thought about that before I ran away? My life was going to change drastically, not having servants to do everything for me. I moved further into the kitchen, studying what he was doing. If I was going to learn to do things for myself, I might as well start now.

The tips of his fingers were still reddened from the weather as he held up two cans, flashing them at me. "Chicken Noodle or Vegetable?"

"Chicken is great." I pulled both of my brows up, gesturing toward the cupboard, trying to figure out how to be useful in the kitchen. "I can set out dishes—" I nervously rubbed my neck as my eyes drifted over to the tiny kitchen with no table. "Where do you eat?"

"Right." His T was extra sharp as he dumped the can into the pot and carried it to the fire. In my search for the table, I had missed him opening the can. I hadn't heard any power tools. Did it just pop open?

"Secret's out," he said in his teasing voice. "I'm a bachelor, and I eat right on the sofa."

"Perfect." I gave him a dismissive wave, careful not to show how out-of-place I felt being part of the cooking process. I shuffled my feet back toward the couch since I didn't find anything to do in the kitchen.

He was quiet as he lifted the cast iron pot with the handle, and carried it to the fireplace, adding another two logs to the already roaring blaze. He clearly wasn't one for small talk, but it was comfortable.

I arched my neck, peering down the hall. "Did you say you have a bathroom?" I filled in a beat with a deliberate blink.

"I dooo." He stretched the word to have three syllables while his eyes seeded with humor. "But remember the no-plumbing?" His gaze drifted through the window to the snow-covered deck.

"Oh." I stiffened. I obviously loved nature, so that didn't bother me, but it was a complete blanket of snow. "So, just head out outside?"

"There are some trees you can squat behind." He chuckled as if he was enjoying my fish-out-of-water predicament, but I couldn't see his expression because he was still turned toward the fire, adjusting his pot.

"Right." I inched toward the door, clamping down on my bottom lip as this conversation strengthened my urge. "It's like camping." I forced a positive tone, as I slipped on my shoes. When I stood up straight, Reeves had managed to move in right next to me and offered his heavy coat. I took it, smiled at his conscientiousness, and placed a hand on the doorknob. "So...just trek on out and find a spot?"

"The world is your oyster." He playfully winked at me as if he was enjoying this too much, but the spark that seeded in the corner of his eye made my breath rush in unexpectedly. I didn't ever remember being affected like this just being near someone. Or maybe it was just my need to pee?

"You mean bathroom," I managed to joke back.

"That too." He jerked his thumb over his shoulder toward the kitchen. "And I'll start the water for coffee on the fire, too."

"That would be lovely." Turning the knob, I didn't even have to pull the door back, because the wind was so strong, it flung the door at me. Gritting my teeth into the gusts, I plowed forward, pulling the door shut behind me. "This will be fun."

I surveyed the yard, deciding that proximity would be my friend. My eyes landed on a pine tree a few strides away. The tree was near, but the snow was almost waist high, and I struggled to move forward. My legs sank deep into each footstep of snow. My teeth chattered together as the snow filled my shoes, burning my feet. *This was awful.* I don't even know what the point of squatting is because the snow was so high, when I pulled my skirt up, my bare bum touched the snow. Still, I tried to stay positive, as I closed my eyes and squeezed. It was only a minute and it'd be all over. There wasn't an angle that was graceful, and no matter how I leaned, I couldn't stop the pee from getting on my shoe. If only Father knew what I was doing now. He'd immediately rush me back to etiquette school. This was disgusting, but it was done.

I gave myself a mental pat on the back. As I stood to fix my dress, a gust of wind rustled up the tree branches. It was almost like time had been put into slow motion as I saw the spiral ripple through the tree. I didn't react fast enough before an enormous mound of snow rolled off the top branch. Throwing my hands up in protection, it was obviously a feeble attempt at coverage that failed, and the mass plummeted directly on my head. I squealed as the pile dissected and snow trickled over my whole body, freezing me still.

Shaking from the cold, I strained to brush it away, while running toward the house, desperate to get warm. I rounded the tree, my eyes met Reeves, who was standing on the deck. He had a rascal smile on his face, as if he was dying to make fun of me.

"Not funny." I stomped the snow off my shoes as I trekked across the deck.

"I heard you scream. I thought a coyote had got you." He stood back, allowing me to go indoors first, still chuckling through his words. "I think you're going to need to change. I don't have anything your size, but I can get you a sweat-shirt and some shorts."

My eyes regarded the coat, layered in wet snow. I could easily remove that but the whole bottom of my skirt had been layered in snow from traipsing through it. There was no way I could brush it clean. It would only take a minute in the warmth of this cabin, and it would be soaked. Clearly, I hadn't thought out this running-away-on-foot thing, as I could have used at least one change of clothes. Without another option, I relented. "That would be great."

"Come back here." He led the way to his bedroom. I maintained a straightforward stare, trying not to snoop, but I was curious. You can tell a lot from a person's room. Even though he had recently moved in, it was apparent he'd tried to make it his own. The single window had blackout curtains and a blue blanket on the wood-framed bed. The bed was neatly made—military corners—and I gave him huge props for that. On the side table, he had a set of earbuds, a wireless phone charger, and a Bible. A large dark wood dresser sat across the room, the top space bare except for a small fan. "Here." He laid his items on the corner of the bed and went straight to the door, calling back, "Let me know if they don't work."

With shivers still trembling through me, I slipped off my dress as quickly as I could and picked up his sweatshirt. The inside was a soft fleece that was cozy against my skin. As I grabbed his shorts, a blush hit my cheeks. I stepped into them and then padded back to the living room, the aroma of strong coffee leading the way.

Reeves already had two bowls of soup waiting on the counter.

"Thank you." I reached out and cupped a bowl with both of my hands, and brought it close to my body, the heat warming me. With one eye steady on my filled-to-the-brim bowl that was steaming out of the center, I headed to the sofa. I don't think I'd ever eaten anything that came from a can before. I wouldn't really know as we always had chefs at the palace, but I went an entire day yesterday without a bite to eat, and I was famished. Nothing ever looked more delicious to me in my life.

Reeves retrieved the other bowl and casually took the spot on the couch next to me. "Sorry about the seating arrangements. I wasn't planning on having company."

"Don't apologize." I lifted my spoon, scooped up a noodle, and held it up, letting it steam. "I'm sorry about my intrusion. You must know this wasn't my plan."

"I don't mind." As he lifted his hand to eat, his arm brushed against mine, and it left prickles that spiraled up my arm.

Sitting with Reeves was not uncomfortable, but he was always so quiet, and the silence expanded enough to make me risk small talk. "How much snow did we get?"

"A little over sixteen inches so far, but it's supposed to pick up again this morning and bring another foot today. With the wind, it will be a complete whiteout again." He dabbed the corner of his mouth with a napkin. "You won't be going anywhere for at least another day."

"That might be okay." I considered the timeframe as I spoke. "It will give me time to come up with a plan."

His brows furrowed together, pinning a confused look in place. "You don't know what you're doing?"

"Do I ever?" I flashed a look heavenward. "I obviously didn't plan any of this. I'd been preparing my heart for engagement, but this feeling of betrayal enveloped my heart." I paused, taking time to swallow, even though there wasn't any food in my mouth. It was the swelling that came whenever I pictured sweet Weston on the frontlines. Yeah, he was a trained infantry soldier, but never a fighter. He went into the military with the sole intention of being my personal guard because Father had already laid the offer on the table. It was known from the start that Weston was always to be at the palace, and never in danger. It was a way for him to earn money right out of school, without having to go from home. And don't get me started on his poor, single mother. She had to be beside herself. As far as I was concerned, Father betrayed us all.

"You could go to America." His expression was indifferent.

I hadn't thought about going that far, but it made sense once the words were out. I couldn't hang around here where I could be recognized. As I scooped up the last of my soup, I pictured myself walking on an American city street, blending into the crowd. I could get a job in some office, maybe as an assistant or something. Nobody would ever suspect a princess would work that kind of job. I'd wear those high-rise trousers that I always see American businesswoman wearing on TV, with white button shirts. I could easily cut my long hair into something that's perceived to be more professional. It could work. "I've never been there. Have you?"

"A few times." He reached over and took my empty bowl from me, returning our dishes to the sink. It hadn't dawned on me until that moment that perhaps I was supposed to take care of my own bowl. I'd never cleared a dish in my life. I wasn't even sure what you did with them when they left the table. He put them in the sink. Did you air them out for a while? I would assume you'd need soap . . .

"Do you want coffee?" He cut off my train of thought, by flashing the coffee pot at me.

"I'm good, thank you." I brought my feet up in front of my body, curling into a ball while pondering on the idea of

America. "If I went to America," I rubbed the back of my neck, speaking as the thoughts came. "I'd have to fly and could be tracked. Unless do you have a way—"

"I wasn't special intelligence." He snickered as if he was reading my mind, but after a moment of silence he had some suggestions. "You'd have to get a fake ID to travel commercially. Or, if you have the money, you can risk paying someone off." He held a serious expression as if this was an average conversation, but that grated on my conscience. Clearly, he'd been through some stuff, but disappearing and faking identities shouldn't have been such an easy conversation for anyone. I considered it, but it felt so far-fetched, I had a hard time not giggling. It was absurd. His ability to have this conversation, and not be affected, made me curious about him.

Whenever we were together, I was the one who did most of the talking. I didn't know much about him. "So, the Army," I echoed, taking the rare chance since he brought it up. "What was that like?"

"Sucked." His one-word answer slammed the door on that conversation.

"Care to expand?" I winced at how not smooth that sounded, and I was glad he was standing behind me.

"Nope."

"You have to have gained something from it." I cringed, wondering why I was forcing this when it was clear he didn't want to talk about it. The thing is, I was curious. With Weston on the frontlines, I was terrified of all the things that were happening. Maybe I was wanting Reeves to say it was the best experience and you're never scared. It was silly because I wasn't naive about war. I was grasping for hope that maybe . . . someday, I'd see Weston again. I was also insanely curious about his hand, something that was always there but he never talked about. I turned, peering over my shoulder, hoping to glimpse at his facial expression or anything that would help me better to understand everything.

"It's one thing you're glad about when it ends." As if he couldn't risk even another prying question, he moved toward the door and slipped on his coat. "I'm going to check on my animals."

My brows knitted together. I had hit a nerve, and now I felt awful. I wasn't trying to upset him, but I wanted to know something about him other than what was obvious. "Sorry," the word burst out.

He folded his bottom lip under as he gripped the doorframe and slipped on his boots. "I'm fine not talking about me."

My lips fell apart as I now had this nagging guilt. I pinched my words as he placed his hat on his head, nodded his goodbye, and left.

Bringing my thumb to my mouth, I chewed on the tip of my thumbnail as I watched through the window. I thought about how he forced me to dance with him at the festival. He had seemed so charismatic that night, so different. Almost as if he were playing a character role of some sort. Today, he slipped back into a somber tone. He was hard to place. Definitely moody. It was clearly two different people.

A chameleon. Though I could understand his need for different facades, that made me nervous. Who was he really, and why did it seem as if he was trying to be someone he wasn't sometimes?

It's almost like he's up to something.

Fifteen

Reeves

Trekking through some snow drifts, and over the tops of some of the more compact piles, I traipsed to the barn. Unfortunately, the old-style red barn had fared even worse than my rundown house as the whole structure seemed off-balance. If I listened hard enough, I could hear it creak under the pressure of the snow. I had joked when I first saw this barn, that one good storm would blow it away. I trod carefully into the open space, hoping today wasn't the day I would test that theory.

I was anxious to build a new home next summer for Hank, my Friesian horse. Hank was twenty years old and had come with the property. I saw his age as a bonus more than a liability, because he was smart, more intelligent than most horses I'd ever owned. Even though we'd only been family for the last week, I could tell he liked me. This was evident by how he willingly left his place guarding his oat bucket to meet me halfway.

"Wind's blowing today, boy." I patted his snout and grinned at the way he showed me his giant teeth. I could stand here all day if I didn't have anything else to do. He was just an easy keeper. "Do you need some treats?" I strode to the sacks, easily found his favorite oat blend, and carried it back to his bucket. He moved behind me, watching me with giant eyes as I filled his bucket. "We have company today," I filled him in. "A princess."

I moved the bucket closer to him, and he didn't waste a minute pushing his snout in. "I know what you're thinking. A *real* princess?" I nodded to myself. "Yep. A real princess." I tsked, as if I was in pain. "Tell ya what, she looks amazing in my shirt."

I threw my head back, slamming my eyes to the heavens.

Stop thinking about that, Reeves! Get a grip. She's a princess! She's only being nice to you because you're marooned together. Give it another day, and she'll be on her way.

And that's the craziest thought of all.

Just how fragile this whole situation was.

I had to stay focused and see it as it was, or I would suffer in the long run. She wasn't here to fall in love with me.

Or is she?

She has this habit where she rubs her neck when she's deep in thought. The first time I saw her do that, it was in my field and her expression was wistful, as if she was lost in a fantasy world. The last couple of days, her face has been pinched, and serious. Either way, I just stare at her hand and daydream, wondering what it would feel like to press a kiss into her neck.

And there I go again!

Stop. Don't even think about her. I slammed my gaze to the ceiling beams. Think about something else. Anything but her. Gotta stay busy.

I rolled up the sack, sealing it as best as I could, and set it out of Hank's reach because I'd already made the mistake of leaving it open with him once.

There. I brushed my hands on my jeans, looking around for something else to do. This chore did nothing to take my mind off of her. If anything, it had only filled it further. I passed back out the barn door, pulling it closed. The wood had long since been warped and didn't match in the middle seam the way it should, but I sealed it as best as I could, and secured the latch.

I flicked my gaze to the clouds, praying for the sun. Sun was the only way I was getting myself out of this close-encounter predicament. As soon as this storm passes, she'd be gone.

All I saw was gray looming clouds, threatening to dump out more snow.

Pulling my single glove out of my coat pocket, I slipped it on. I had plenty of chores to keep me busy, including feeding my cows. The tractor had a heater, and plenty of fuel. It would give me a place to hang out without the distraction . . . Yeah, it sounded like a good plan to me.

Avoid the house until dark.

Sixteen

Princess Erralee

With Reeves outside, I couldn't help but watch out the front window, studying him. The window panel had frosted up along most of the outer edges, but there was a perfect circle in the center just large enough for me to peek through. It's funny how you think you know what you want in life, or what you don't want. Then one day something happens, and nothing makes sense . . . Everything you knew to be true has fallen away, leaving a new world you never even considered had existed.

There was a stirring in my heart that had been quickening all morning. As much as I tried to say it was the anxiety over my situation, if I were being honest with myself, I'd have to admit it was Reeves.

Reeves was placed in my life at the exact moment I didn't need a distraction. The way I saw it, my mission had been clear. I had a path carved out, one with two roads. One path to save my country, and the other to blaze alone. That choice had been hard enough, but what was this potential third option? Like a cul de sac, wrapping my emotions, wanting to keep me here... Now, I have this pull. I can't even explain it, but as I look around Reeves' house, and see all these normal everyday things, it almost feels like this is what I've been missing.

I had never considered what life would be like if I hadn't been royal. It was so ingrained in my upbringing, I had never seen anything but the straight path. Maybe my trepidation in marrying King Aswell wasn't as much about him? He has been a perfect gentleman in all ways to me. Now, as I had the distance to consider this, I think I was avoiding the spotlight that would come from being his wife. I had no desire to be a queen, or be put on display. I had never been that girl who wanted fame. Maybe what I needed was just a regular life? Being stuck in Reeves' house presented me with another option.

The irony is that this option would never be an option.

It was just a fantasy.

I paced Reeve's tiny living room, picturing Reeves coming through the front door with the first flowers of spring freshly picked. I imagined us heading out to the fields together, him checking cows, me napping. My mind was reeling through all the things we could do together because we actually had a lot in common. I had more in common with Reeves than anyone in my family. How is it a relationship that doesn't even exist, and isn't an option, is the one that makes the most sense to me?

Reeves finally returned to the house after the sun was already fading. I stepped away from the window, blinking away my thoughts as he pushed through the door. His eyes were wide, but not anxious, as he spoke, "It looks like the plows are out on the main road. You might get out of here sooner than we thought."

He turned his back to me, removing his outerwear, and I was left panicking. There's the knot again. If I'd calmed at all, something shifted again, and suddenly my gut was in my throat. I stole my gaze away, hoping he wouldn't see the panic that was surely seeping onto my face. It had been my plan to run away, but now that I'd been sitting here mulling it over for hours, I wasn't sure where to go, or what to do.

"Ah, look at that," he exclaimed, pointing at the microwave's flashing clock. "The power is back on."

"Yeah." I joined his gaze toward the microwave. "I heard it come on just a few minutes ago."

He crossed the room, setting the time while checking the digits on his wristwatch. "Let's hope it stays on." Turning back to me, his brows knitted together. "Sorry, I was outside so long. I wanted to get as much snow moved as possible before dark. How are you?"

"I rested most of the day, watched out the window—" I tried to brush his apology away, but he spoke over top of me.

"I wasn't asking what you *did*. I knew there was nothing to do. I asked how you *are*." His brows angled down in a manner that commanded me not to dismiss his question. It's as if he suddenly had a special power to see through me. I didn't have a choice but to be honest.

I didn't dare tell him how I was massively confused and rethinking everything. I didn't understand how I'd been single forever. Now that I was engaged, I found zero at-traction to the man, but I got weak in the knees when I was near another. I also didn't dare tell him I felt the attraction seed days ago, but being stuck here with him made my mind wander in the most curious ways. I never saw him with another woman. I didn't think he was playing me by buying me roses. Nothing added up.

I also didn't tell him that once again, I was scared to run away. My mind had been awakened to the fact that I knew nothing about how to take care of myself. My brain was a pool of confusion, and as the silence expanded it was so loud it eventually drowned out all my thoughts, and we were left standing there. Heat flushed my skin, and my fake smile was brittle.

He paced a step closer, lowering his gaze as if he was looking for physical signs of illness. Still, no words were spoken, and I watched him watch me. It was as if we were dancing without touching; an invisible deafening void of audible words rang so loud, it made my knees weaker with each breath. I felt as if he could see right through me. "I'm fine," I finally murmured with weakened breath, completely aware of the effect of his heated glare.

As if he couldn't handle standing in the pulsating silence for another moment, he tore his gaze from me and moved to the cupboard again. "I don't trust anything in the fridge anymore." He pursed his lips and grabbed a box of pasta and some marinara sauce. "How about Italian?"

"That's perfect," I breathed out, wondering why some-thing so simple as dinner plans suddenly made me feel as if my heart was on display. It was an odd sort of date, that wasn't a date. Forced dinner together. It was the nearness to him. Seeing him at home, doing everyday things. Who would think cooking with someone would feel like this? How did I not know what normal life was until now? It was more intimate than expected, allowing me to see the real him.

Even if I didn't want it, he was probably getting a dose of the average me. Someone nobody ever got to see. I never went anywhere without dresses, hair, and the royal façade. My father would hit the ceiling if he saw me standing in this kitchen wearing some guy's shirt.

But strangely, it felt more right than anything I'd ever experienced. I pulled on my lips, hoping to crease them enough into something that could pass for a smile. It wasn't that I was unhappy, because there was a seed of something so light and giddy in my chest, I couldn't deny it. Unfortunately, there was an underlying knot swelling too, competing for attention.

Don't even think about Reeves. It's an impossibility. My father will have both of our heads.

Seventeen

Reeves

One bonus to all this snow, it brought a clean water source right to my step. I carried our pasta—which I made with melted snow water—to the couch. It was good enough for me, but I'd never entertained royalty before, and the improvisation made me feel like total riffraff.

Ever since I had returned from chores, Erralee had acted a little out of character. I told myself she was nervous about her move, but she kept looking at me, parting her lips, as if there was something deeper. Maybe it was my imagination—or even my desire—but I'd seen that look before. Not from Erralee, but from another woman I'd dated. Sure, it'd been a while, but it's the sort of look you didn't forget.

I kept checking out the window, hoping to see the snow stop. *I need her gone.* I was out of my mind to invite her to stay here. It's not like I had an option not to invite her. It was an emergency. However, seeing her in my kitchen, and snuggling in on my sofa, brought thoughts into my head, that in normal circumstances would be fine.

Attraction is fine.

Normal.

Attraction to a woman who is engaged is not good.

In this situation, that attraction would be lethal.

Erralee is off-limits.

My scowl grew as the wind had picked up. Again. Snow flooded out of the clouds all at once, as if someone had pulled a giant plug. I glared out the window, praying for a sunray. Nature only mocked me with a huge blast of snow slamming the window, making it impossible to see out.

"Mmm." I grinded down on my bottom lip. I was going to suffer dearly for this. *It's just a crush.* I took my first bite of pasta, swallowed, and forced small talk. "It's going to snow until around midnight, then it should let up. If they keep the roads open, you should be able to leave tomorrow."

Her chin tilted away from me. I immediately realized how that sounded like I was rushing her. "But you don't have to leave," I added quickly. "I'm not forcing you out."

But you really do need to leave . . . soon.

"I do." She hovered her fork above her bowl. "I'm surprised Father hasn't had someone come by already. He's not usually one to take being crossed lightly. Hence this stupid two-year war."

My conscience was conflicted in so many ways. She was capable, and resourceful. I disagreed with what her father had done. She had a right to live her life, but I doubted she understood she was putting herself in danger by running away. People might end up hating her, once everything comes to light. As I thought about the violence people were capable of, my pulse quickened. I was afraid for her. "But you still don't know where you are going to go, do you?"

"Yeah." She swallowed her pasta, and tacked on, "You were right about America."

"Okaaay," I stretched the word out to make it a complete sentence. Her innocence about everything was a bit perturbing. "And how will you get there without blowing your cover?"

"I'm telling you this in confidence." She leaned closer, even though we were the only two people. "I'm going to leave at night, and go to Weston's mom's house. She used to be my nanny, and to be honest, I trust her more than my parents. I'm going to have her lend me Weston's birth records, and some clothes for a disguise. We're the same age and height. I can cut and dye my hair. Then I'll take his records to get a photo ID and use that to fly commercially. If I know Father, he would have checked with her already. So, I'm sure her place is clear—"

"Unless—" I cut in, "He's expecting you to come eventually, and he's watching it."

She held up a point-making finger. "That would make sense, but he doesn't have the resources. He's already down a guard at the palace, and his military is gone."

I hike a brow northerly, pressing my concern. "But King Aswell is not out of resources."

Her pupils shifted from side to side. "What are you saying?"

"I'm saying I don't know this guy, but most men aren't going to let what's theirs just get away or be taken from them. If he really has the army you say he has, he might use it to find you, and fight for you."

"I hadn't thought of that." She ran a hand through her hair, appearing to redirect her thoughts. "I know Weston's mom will help me. It's the only way forward, but I need to find a way to meet with her covertly. As you said, she might be getting surveilled." Her eyes trailed slowly to mine. "Do you—"

"You want me to reach out to her?" I jerked my thumb to my chest. "Do you know what the punishment is for treason?"

A serious line pinned between her eyes, while she kept an even tone. "It can't be worse than harboring me here."

"Thanks for reminding me of that." I half-laughed, half-scoffed. I had no idea how I got sucked into this drama. "I'm not harboring you. In case you have forgotten I rescued you."

"Look," She reached forward, dropping her palm to my leg, and an electric shock zapped right through me. I jolted into a more upright position with my gaze landing on her hand on my leg. I wasn't sure how this transitioned into a touching situation, but now my mind was going in a new direction. "I appreciate your friendship so much," her words drowned out the tingles I still had. "I'm sorry to put you through this, but I can't marry a man I don't love." Her heated gaze paced my face. "I'm not asking for anything that anyone else isn't allowed. I want the freedom to live my life. I shouldn't have fewer rights because I was born into this family. I should get to love who I want."

It was a cause I understood, but there was deep naivety in her thinking. Plus, her hand was still on my leg, which made any sort of rational thinking impossible. I'd had a lot of misfortune in my life, and many things happened that I'd never understand, but how I got stranded with the most beautiful woman in the world—who happens to be a princess—*and* is totally off-limits will now be on the top of my why-do-all-the-insanely-impossible-things-happen-to-me list.

I didn't want to make her sad or stressed out, as I didn't see the point of worrying about this stuff when the unknown was just that . . . unknown. I placed my hand on top of hers, fully intending that's where it would stay.

Stationary.

Friendly support.

Like a pat on the back.

She immediately flipped her hand over, enveloping her fingers in mine. Maybe she was one of those overly touchy-feely people who had no sense of personal space, but the vibe I was getting...made it feel more intentional than that.

Or maybe I was hoping?

But that could be bad, because she was off-limits.

King Aswell could *kill* me.

I didn't want to die!

"Put it this way," I said, finally mustering up a response, as I casually slipped my hand back, and stood returning my bowl to the sink. "I'm not going to let anything bad happen to you, but let's not waste our evening worrying about it." I bobbed my head toward the TV. "The power's back on. It's been a long day. We should relax and watch a movie."

That way, we don't have to talk to each other, and we can stare at a screen. Perfect diversion to get through the night.

Her gaze wafted toward the mounted flat screen. "What do you have?"

"I don't know if the streaming is going to work the best." I exhaled noisily. The noise wasn't on purpose. That apparently just happened when I'm flustered. I walked back to the living room, grabbed the remote, and clicked it on. Several channels weren't coming in, but we had a few choices. "So, it looks like we have the National News Channel, Christmas Movie Channel, or infomercials."

"Oh, I love Christmas movies." She immediately gushed, and I realized I had made a massive miscalculation. Christmas movies were *date* movies. Sure, it would take her mind off her problems, but it felt risky. "Ah, are you sure you're not tired? Maybe we should just go to sleep." I eyed my bedroom door, wondering how suspicious that would look if I just turbo tiptoed in there and barricaded the door until she left.

"No, I napped while you did chores." She had this sensational smile on her face, like it alone was proof that she wasn't tired.

"Okaay." I clicked on the Christmas Movie Channel and dropped the remote. My gaze went back to the sofa. The *one* sofa I had in this house. I never thought having only one piece of furniture would be the wrong decision. That was before I had an Erralee sitting on it, batting her lashes at me like she was getting her own ideas.

I backed up, until my heels bumped into the front of the sofa. I was committed to not locking eyes with her. I sat on the edge of the couch, upright as if I was so engrossed in the opening credits, I couldn't take my eyes off the screen for a second.

"There's a bit of a glare from the kitchen light behind us. I can't see this part of the screen." She stretched her neck up, scanning the room. "Do you have a switch for that light?"

"Yep." I popped the P as I stiffly stood, doing my best to sidestep and avoid her gaze. I flipped the switch and resumed my position. Now we were sitting way too close in the dark, and my skin prickled from her gaze hovering over it. My entire life, I was the guy who struggled to get the girl. I'd ask for a date, and so many times they'd have an excuse. You could have never told me that one day, I'd be on this accidental date with the most desired woman on the planet, and there'd be a giant BUT.

BUT . . . she's off limits.

BUT she keeps looking at me as if she wants to flirt.

BUT her father could very well punish me for making a move on his daughter.

BUT I wasn't sure I cared about her dad now.

BUT her fiancé could very well kill me for even thinking about her.

BUT at this moment the only thing I cared about was the way she was looking at me.

BUT she was a princess.

What kind of flex did I have? Nada that could measure up to that.

I sat on my corner of the couch.

She sat on hers.

It was cozy.

Er, who was I kidding, I was sweating like I was in a sauna, fighting for my life not to look at her, even though I could feel her eyes on me. I wasn't super intelligent. I had an IQ north of ninety. However, if there was anything I had ever been one-thousand percent sure of, it was that if we locked eyes, even for a second, I'd lose all willpower.

For all these buts, and more, I crossed my arms over my chest, sank down on the couch, and *focused* on the movie as if my life depended on it.

Because it did.

Eighteen

Princess Erralee

Giggling to myself at the oddly proper manner Reeves was exhibiting, he'd clearly done a one-eighty since I first met him. The only logical reason for his transformation had to be this budding attraction we'd been experiencing. At first, I thought it was in my head, but the second I had batted my lashes at him, and smiled flirtatiously, he'd become a fumbling, clumsy, yet adorable and attractive man.

I didn't have a clue what was happening in this movie, because I was too entertained watching him sweat, and pretend to care about this chick flick. I made him uncomfortable, but that wasn't fair. I had to believe that it was my situation that was the bigger issue. Not knowing how to bring it up because contrary to what people would think about an available princess, I'd never really had a boyfriend. Men were always scared of me. Or maybe they were scared of my father, but either way, I'd never been in a situation where I was alone with a guy I had a crush on, and he was clearly attracted to me too.

I didn't even have a guard looking over my shoulder.

I'd *never* been without Weston.

This whole running away thing was about me taking control of my destiny. If I fully commit to that, I should be capable of letting an adorably sweet man know that I'm attracted to him.

I just didn't know *how*.

I tried the subtle hints of holding his hand, but I think it was a little too subtle because he seemed to have brushed that off as a friendly gesture. The movie was almost over, and our time would be up tomorrow. Was it terrible that I wanted to experience my first crush? I was almost twenty.

But this felt like a crowded bus.

He was so stiff, and I could hear his measured breathing get louder, as if I was bothering him.

"Reeves," I whispered with an insane amount of attraction seeding my voice. I couldn't contain it, not sitting this close to him. My breath just wanted to rush in and out of my lungs like I was playing a sport.

His gaze slid slowly toward me, with his brows commanding me to explain what I was up to. When I didn't say anything, his gaze softened. Then instantly heated, and I was frozen.

He tucked a stray hair back behind my ear, and the mere brush of his skin against mine, left me breathless. The silence expanded, and for the first time, I didn't feel I needed to fill it in with chatter.

"Erralee," my name rumbled out of his mouth in the deepest octave. It was raspy, and held a warning, almost like an apology pleading minutes before an offense.

Leaning closer, I raised my chin, parting my lips slowly, waiting for his. He moved toward me, and just when I thought we'd kiss, he dropped his lips to my neck and whispered, "You aren't mine to kiss. If I kiss you, I'm going to want to keep you."

My heart slammed against my ribcage, motoring away at top speeds.

I wanted him to keep me, and I raised my chin, but he turned his head a heart-wrenching angle away, before he got up and went to his room, shutting the door between us. It was a cruel punishment that the first time that I felt a real crush, it wasn't reciprocated.

Nineteen

Reeves

I was the biggest jerk for not kissing her.

I wasn't sure if the pounding in my chest was the excitement of the attraction, the anger about my failure, or a flat-out heart attack.

Part of me wished it was a heart attack so I would *not* have to face her again.

Or King Aswell with his army.

I didn't want to explain to her how I couldn't handle being in the room with her for even another five minutes.

I knew my limitations. If I kissed her, I'd pay for it for the rest of my life. And maybe it would have been worth it? Maybe that would be a highlight I could brag about when I'm eighty.

The day I kissed a princess!

But I wasn't who she needed.

She was off-limits.

I could be wrong.

Maybe I was wrong.

Could I be wrong?

I shut my eyes and rubbed my temple, trying to tamp down the pressure. There's no way anything would ever work between us.

We were stir crazy from being cooped up together for so long.

Yeah, that's it.

It would be better in the morning.

I flattened out on my bed, letting my hands rest behind my head and forced my eyes to close. Just one more night and she's gone tomorrow.

"There he is!" King Aswell unsheathed his sword, pushing the tip to my neck. "You thought you could get away with stealing my bride." He threw his head back and laughed the cruelest of laughs. I didn't dare move because I was pinned. He jabbed the tip of his sword into my neck.

Drip. Drip. Drip.

Frigid drops plucked down on my neck, springing me awake, and I jolted to an upright position. Panting, my thoughts popped in my head like fireworks.

It was another nightmare.

Water was falling from the ceiling.

I'm not being executed. Only drowned!

That's the best news ever!

I grabbed my chest, my shirt soaked all the way through, but not from roof water. It was clearly hot sweat. I slipped off my shirt, but still didn't settle. Instead, a cough tore up my burning lungs, and my eyes glued to my bedroom door. I needed water to drink, but she was out there.

She had to be sleeping.

I doubted it was even midnight, and the wind was muffled outside as if it was finally getting farther away. I could be stealthy and sneak into the kitchen, grab a bottle of water, and be back before she heard me.

Before I talked myself out of it, I headed out. One step inside the living room, I halted on my heel. Erralee was sitting completely upright on the couch staring blankly at the TV, a late news show was on. The sound was muted, but closed captions were scrolling along the bottom. Clearly, she was not asleep. I slid my foot backward, but it was too late. She spotted me, and she gave me a look I didn't need.

One that pulled me to her.

"Water," I coughed out, pacing to the fridge. I retrieved a bottle and downed most of it in one pull. "Need one?" I huffed out as I came up for air and her eyes were still locked on me. *Is she looking at me like that just because she knows it affects me?*

"Sure," she eagerly accepted, sounding way too awake.

"Here you go." I tossed one underhand, and spun on my heel, eyes focused on my bedroom door. "Back to bed—"

"Reeves," she cut in, her voice sounding more urgent than usual.

I made the mistake of letting my gaze sweep to her as she pulled a stray hair over her shoulder. Even through my sleepy haze, she seemed to have a magnetic force drawing me in. This roommate experiment was going to be the death of me. I couldn't survive if every time I came out of my room, I'd have to pretend to be indifferent to her presence. I'd rather take my chances sleeping in the dilapidated barn.

"What do you need?" I answered like I was talking to my drill sergeant, even clicking my heels together out of habit.

"I don't *need* anything." Her hair was swept over one shoulder, and she anxiously twirled the end of it with her fingers. "I can't sleep."

"Err, maybe open a window, and get some fresh air?" I darted to the living room window, grateful to have any-thing to do that meant I didn't have to look at her. I cracked the window enough to feel the rush of cold air while I scanned the sky for signs of dawn. Nothing but black sky for miles. My legs were itching in urgency to go outside and get away. *I could fake an emergency*. Before I had time to think up something, she stalled me.

"How do you make decisions?" she huffed out as if all her potential prospects were terrible.

I slowly moved, peered back to her and saw a glimmer of hope I hadn't seen in days resurrected in her eyes, compelling me to take her concerns seriously. However, I wasn't going to budge. I couldn't risk getting any closer. I leaned against the wall, crossing my arms over my chest. "What do you mean?"

"I've never been allowed to decide anything. Now that I'm no longer allowing my father to dictate my future—" She wagged her head back and forth as if that would fill in the rest of her thoughts before gesturing toward me. "You have this whole life that was your idea. How'd you do it?"

"I always knew I wanted to serve my country. That was non-negotiable for me." My lips twitched, as I mulled over my life, but oddly, they landed on a smile. "Neither was my decision to farm. After being in war, I wanted a normal boring life. I wanted to wake up every day, and know I'd have the same reliable coffee in the same mug. I would do the same things every day, and trust that, at the end of the day, I'd have the same bed to sleep in at night. After living with so much uncertainty while at war, all I wanted was stability. Eventually, with time I want a family." My smile inflated, tacking on. "I think the family will be the best part."

Her nose wrinkled at the top as she pulled her lips into a small grin. "I didn't know you wanted kids."

Why is my brow suddenly beading with sweat when I'm standing next to an open window in winter? Surely it had nothing to do with the pining look she was flashing at me. "Yeah, it's not something I'm actively thinking about right now." I tossed up a shoulder, trying to downplay how much I'd planned for this next season of life. "I've always wanted a big family. Some people are just born knowing what they want to do."

Her expression went blank, as if she was staring into a void. "I think maybe I was born knowing what I wanted to do, but my father quelled it out of me."

I started to suspect this conversation had two meanings. On the surface, we were talking about her life, but with the way she was looking at me, I wondered if she was trying to ask me something else. Something that made me suffer deeply. "It's not too late to get it back." I speak softly, a little afraid of the direction this conversation is going.

Her brows were raised in preparation for her question. "How do I do that?"

"Just ask yourself what *you* want to do?"

"I think I want a normal life too." She shifted in her seat as if my words made her uncomfortable. "That would take a miracle."

We were interrupted by my phone alert, echoing from my bedroom. I was still in a few army calling trees for first responder notifications. It always felt good being first to find things out about any emergencies. Sometimes it was annoying. But with Erralee's dear friend, Weston, on the frontline, I darted to the bedroom and grabbed for my phone.

Emergency news update: King D'Long was treated for a heart attack at his home and is now being airlifted to the hospital. The Queen asks for prayers for him, as well as asking for reports on the whereabouts of Princess Erralee, who is still missing.

My heart hammered inside my chest. If Erralee had been wavering before, this would have put her over the edge. I couldn't keep it from her. I crossed the room again, but I didn't need to show it to her. The soft light of the glowing TV filled the room with closed captions flashing across the bottom with the same emergency news bulletin.

"I did this," she breathed out in a voice so weak, it was as if any sound would break her chest. "My father's dying, and it is surely some heavenly atonement for my sins. If I could have predicted something like this would happen, I would never have left," she rambled as tears flooded her eyes and a tremor of panic must have shot through her, because everything from her fingers to her jaw shook with little flutters. "Clearly the stress of this war—this never-ending brutality that *I* could have stopped—has finally come to claim him," she went on as if she was presenting an argument to herself. Her tone was getting harsher with each word. "Not to mention the added pain of finding me gone, and then having to break the lifesaving covenant he had tried so hard to obtain." Her hand found her chest, as if holding her heart would stabilize the pressure she felt as she fused her argument. "That was all on me. I have to go home to fix this before it's too late. It's all my fault."

"You didn't know." Dying inside to see her upset, I stepped closer, closing the gap between us. Even though she was standing, I could feel a weakness encapsulating her frame. Maybe I had a premonition, but I reached out, just as she collapsed into my arms, sobbing as if it was the antidote to cure her dad.

I dropped my face into her neck, inhaling her. It wasn't the proper time, but I understood she'd go back without hesitation. This was the lightning bolt that brought us both back to reality, putting us in our proper places. But before I let her go, I needed just one selfish minute to tattoo her scent, her essence onto my heart, and I selfishly held her. When her cries softened, I dropped my gaze to hers. "I'll drive you home in the tractor. If you stay here any longer, I will fall in love with you, and we both know that can't happen."

Her eyelids quivered as if she was absorbing a bullet to the heart, and her breath audibly hitched in her chest. It took every ounce of strength I had to pull away, knowing exactly how she'd whither in that marriage. It wasn't what I wanted for her. If it had been up to me, I'd beg her to stay, and promise her the normal life that she said she wanted. I could give her that much. It was what we both wanted, but it didn't matter.

Everything we wanted had fallen away.

Twenty

Princess Erralee

Three months later

"I told you they'd love you." Jon's smile grew, overflowing with pride. I was getting used to his new chin sprout of facial hair. I wouldn't say it was better than his clean-shaven look. Different. It did make his face appear extra elongated, and he tended to look quite crescent moon shaped to begin with. I was okay with it though. Getting used to it. Mostly.

I took slow, intentional strides out of the motorcade car, until Jon wrapped an arm around me, pulling me to his side. One thing about him, he always looked for a way to show his affection in gentlemanly ways. It was sweet. I was getting used to that too. We paused, waving at the sprawling—and still growing—crowd of people cheering outside the palace. It was really endearing. Some people had signs held high over their heads that said, "Welcome" and "We love you!" It was heartwarming to see how many families had brought all their perfectly dressed children out, even on a school day.

This was a huge event for this country as they hadn't had a queen since King Aswell took the throne twenty years ago. Frankly, sometimes I wondered about that, and why he stayed single so long. I hadn't yet found anything grossly alarming about him, other than he'd spend an inhuman amount of time reading. As in locked in a room for days, unless I requested to see him. He was always good about taking my requests, and I never doubted I was his first priority.

I was adjusting to this new life. Already tired of waving, I switched hands. I had fans at home, but not like this. "We just pulled up. How'd they even know I'd be here?"

"The engagement announcement your father released last week alerted the media. We've had press vans swarming the palace ever since."

We moved together, intentionally pacing slower toward the grand palace entrance. This was my first time seeing my new home. It was a commanding structure with thick gray walls, reminding me more of a fortress than the palace I was used to. The windows were tiny, square holes without one balcony in sight. If I had been approaching this building alone, I actually would have been fearful of what was inside. It was so dark and devoid of anything green or alive. Today, my stomach didn't even churn as we crossed the stone walkway adorned with large gargoyles on each side. I had no jitters, as those had seemed to run out days ago. Maybe the stillness inside me was what happened when you finally grew up and left fairytales behind.

I felt nothing.

I saw the nothingness as God's gift. The stillness I needed to fulfill my mission.

Some days I still wondered *why* this was my mission when I didn't seem well suited for it. I'd be lying if I said I didn't wonder why my mission couldn't have been easy, boring and common. A life of common routine.

Other days I tease the fantasy that I never got stuck in a snowstorm. I made my way to America, never having spent that time with Reeves. I never heard about my father's condition, and I was happy working a nine to five. Perhaps I'd have a crush on a barista, or wine boy, who I enjoyed flirting with in the mornings on my way to work. Or maybe ... I'd have gone to an American university to study plants. That's an option I hardly considered, but I didn't doubt it would have brought me joy.

Life had so many options.

Only one mission.

We waved until we passed the final set of guards and entered the palace. The foyer opened up into more matte stone walls and floors, without a tapestry in sight to soften the echo. "Welcome home." Jon's beady eyes were soft as he pressed a kiss to my hand and squeezed my palm in a light caress. "I figured you would be tired tonight, so I didn't plan anything. Just dinner whenever you're ready. Tomorrow, I have a homecoming celebration with every-one you need to meet for the big wedding. It's going to be sensational."

My eyelids drifted down. I was finally here, after weeks of preparing, I felt as if fate was boxing me in. I blinked momentarily, losing focus. "Ah, whatever you feel is best."

He ran his bare knuckle across my forehead and trailed it down my cheek. It took every ounce of my strength not to pull away. "You look tired. Maybe rest before dinner." His gaze skirted behind him, and for the first time I noticed a few staff members waiting in the shadows. A stout woman with a maid's apron, stepped forward, and Jon dutifully directed orders to her. "Mavis, will you take Princess Erralee to her suite and help her settle."

"Yes, Your Excellency." She bowed on her approach. "It's right this way, my lady."

I slipped one foot in front of the other, following her down the long, narrow corridor, until we reached a center door that stuck out as the only white door in the palace. "You'll love your new suite. King Aswell had it prepared just for you." Mavis smiled as if she was holding a secret when she turned the knob, letting me in.

My lips fell agape, while a sweeping breath of fresh air washed through me. All I saw was bright light and clean white. A large four-poster bed sat in the middle of the room, dressed in the most beautiful white linen. Vases of fresh lilacs sat on both nightstands perfuming the air with their sweetness. I wasn't expecting something as pleasant as this, especially after seeing the outside of the palace. This was indeed a sanctuary and best of all . . . there was a large balcony in the corner. I started to make my way to the terrace, but Mavis made a sound that sounded like a hiccup. "Oops, I almost forgot." She pulled out an envelope from her apron and presented it to me. "A card arrived for you yesterday."

My brows pinned together in confusion as I hadn't forwarded any mail here yet, but I received the letter. Before I could ask for privacy, Mavis backed out of the room, calling on her way out, "Just ring the bell if you need anything, my lady."

I didn't immediately recognize the handwriting on the letter, but a quiver ignited in my chest. I'd had my share of congratulations since my engagement went public, and this wasn't the first card I'd received. Still, something about the tiny, boxy scribbles on the front told me this was a different kind of letter.

Careful not to tear it, I ripped the corner first and pulled out a plain card with a fairy dancing on mushrooms on the front. My lips curled for the first genuine time in weeks, and a tear instantly sparked in my eye.

Princess, or dare I say, Queen Erralee:

I was given my discharge orders last night, and although it made no sense to me how I would be relieved of my duties so soon, I knew your hand was on this. The announcement was made this morning to my whole company that we'd all be returning home. . . the opposition pulled out. The war was over.

Obviously, I signed up for this, but as most soldiers do, we quickly find out it's a nightmare we want to end as soon as possible. Everyone here is rejoicing, but I'm sitting here with a heavy heart knowing the sacrifice you made, and wanting to make sure that you understand how brave you are, and your entire country thanks you. My mother will thank you.

I won't return to the palace as you are no longer there. I actually think I might try my luck farming as Reeves offered me a position as his hand.

Forever your guard, Weston

With shaking hands, I let the letter fall to my lap. Weston returning alive was a silver lining that I had hoped for, and one giant blessing I didn't deserve. I'd hold onto it in the coming years, as I desperately tried not to become bitter.

Life has done an excellent job of teaching me the value of detachment.

I'd learned to value the present, while not mourning my past.

Nothing was ever permanently yours.

What ebbed, eventually flowed.

What God giveth, *he could rightfully taketh.*

Today, I was so joyful he didn't take Weston.

Tears pricked the back of my eyes, and everything became worth it. I balled my hand into a fist and covered my heart. *Thank you, Lord, for saving Weston.*

The long hall echoed with emptiness as I found my way to the dining room. My eyes instinctively looked for a window to gaze out, but there was nothing but unending walls, reminding me of a cave. Mavis had said she'd return for me, but when she didn't show up, I figured I'd find my way. Without the chatter of other people to guide my steps, I was hesitant that I was even going in the right direction. I'd never spent time in a home this quiet.

"My dear," Jon's voice pulled from beside me.

I shifted my gaze into an adjacent room where Jon sat looking at me from the head of a long stone table. I slid one foot in front of the other, taking in the hollowness of the room, as it too was devoid of natural light, with a few tall candlesticks glowing in the center. The only other chair was at the opposite end of the table. It was so far away I couldn't imagine having pleasant dinner conversations, because it seemed I'd have to shout. My pulse screamed, begging me to stop this charade. It wasn't too late to go home. I ignored the warning. *Weston was safe. That was enough*. I sank into my seat. That too was stone, without so much as a thin padding.

"Did you have a nice rest?" Jon's voice rose all the way to the cathedral ceiling, and I fought wincing at how uncomfortable this setup was.

"I did." I found my glass of water, already poured for me, and I took a tiny sip. The silence was deafening, grating at my ears. Shouting across this table wasn't ideal, but it was better than the stillness. I swallowed, mustering up small talk. "It's very calm here."

His eyes glistened back at me, as if he was recalling his fond memory. "I love peace. It helps keep my nerves down, like a sanctuary."

More like an asylum.

A staff member padded in through the swinging back door, bringing us our food. I offered her a genuine smile, but she avoided my gaze and left as quietly as she had arrived. I blew out a soft breath, examining my plate. It looked delicious, chicken in some sort of sweet sauce, with rice. I took the tip of my fork and dabbed it into the sauce for a sample. Raspberry with a bit of heat, and it was delicious, but I didn't cut a bite. My stomach had been much too sensitive to take large chunks of food. Jon leaned over his plate, digging in, and I felt envious of his ability to take pleasure in this meal.

Was I ever going to feel pleasure again?

My eyes dampened as my heart deflated. *I had gotten what I wanted.* The war was over. My father was better. He even gave up his nightly scotch in dedication to regaining his health. Weston was alive!

Everything was perfect.

But it wasn't.

I never wanted this royal position. Yes, it was an honor, but I wasn't someone who was into the fanfare. I would gladly give up all this too, if it meant I could just go home. I blinked back tears as Jon's voice cut through the air. "Is something wrong with your food?"

"No, it's lovely." I cleared my throat, hating my heart for not going along with these lies the way my head did. It was going to have to learn to be okay. It will get better. It had to. This was only day one, and I had a whole future to think about. I blew out another even breath.

Just think positively about the future.

"Is there anything you need to be more comfortable?" His voice lowered, pacing consciously.

"No, thank you." I bit down on my lip, screaming at myself to stop making this awkward. This was my new home. *Relax.* "I'm very comfortable," I added before I tacked on, "just noticing how quiet it is here. Do you ever entertain friends?"

His lips tightened into a thin line while he shook his head. "No, not usually."

My gaze wearily floated down, as my mind begged for the silver lining. *The war is over.* I breathed deeply. I was fine the whole time, but reading Weston's letter had somehow opened up my eyes to see that life was going on outside these stone walls, and once again, I was in agony. It was too quiet here. I knew I'd be alone with Jon, but I hadn't anticipated being this alone. *It's only day one,* I breathed. Someday this house will be filled with joyous giggles of small children, and I could laugh reminiscently about how quiet it *used* to be. Then I'd at least have a cute little family to fill my heart.

"Are you sure everything is okay, dear?" Jon's voice treaded delicately, his eyes glued to me.

Lacing my hands together in my lap, I forced a positive conversation, "I was thinking about how lovely it will be when the halls are filled with kids' voices and giggles—"

My voice dropped when his expression soured. He sputtered out a deep cough. I hadn't spent an abundance of time with him, but every time I'd ever seen him, he had a *pleased-to-see-you* smile on his face for me.

"Are you okay?" I was the one who was now concerned.

He balled his hand into a fist, pounding it on his chest a few times as he released more coughs. "Yes, I wasn't expecting you to say that."

"Say what?" I stiffened, afraid I had done something wrong.

"Lots of kids giggling." He chuckled as if he knew he was the last person to solve a punchline. "For a second I thought you were serious."

My lips parted, but no words came out. He was the one who had insisted from the beginning on having an heir. Why would this bother him now? My tiny heart which had been fighting so hard to be strong, cinched together, wringing out the last speck of hope I had been holding onto. Without a family of my own, I'd be stuck in these stone walls withering away. I'd have nothing to look forward to anymore.

His eyes hovered over mine, studious as if he was trying to find the placement of a puzzle piece. After a beat, he tilted his head a measure toward me and said softly, "You can't be serious. I'm almost fifty. I only want one child, a boy. He'll be strong and smart. We'll send him to boarding school because I really don't care to be bothered with the little kid stages."

I held my breath, waiting for my heart to pound harder into the heartbreak, but it stilled. It was as hushed as the walls around me. It had returned to its stillness. A reverie lingered with Jon's eyes still locked on me, widening as if he was getting sickened by something. "Erralee," he repeated firmly. "You're joking about the big family, right?"

Slowly I raised my chin and brought it back down. "Yes, of course I was." A mirage of Reeves flashed in front of my face, telling me that family had to be the best part of life. Why did I have to learn that detail about Reeves? It's like my brain held onto the memory just to taunt me that there was yet another thing that I didn't have in common with my fiancé, but one more thing that lined up perfectly with Reeves.

Reeves was not in my mission.

The following day, Mavis was in my room most of the day, preparing me for the homecoming celebration tonight. "Boy, whoever took your measurements needs glasses." Mavis tugged at the zipper of my gown, doing her best to cinch it tight, but the gown nearly slipped right off me, even once it was fully zipped. "Have you lost weight?"

I stared forward into the full-length mirror, gazing at my body. I hadn't noticed physical changes, but now that she'd pointed it out, I did look quite skinny. My collar bone protruded, and my high cheekbones looked incredibly gaunt. "Maybe." I offered a light toss of the shoulder.

"I will get my sewing kit and add a few stitches, or this gown will never stay up." She took a step back and motioned to the chair. "You look quite frail. Why don't you sit until I get back."

I pivoted slightly, my eyes fleeing to the balcony where I could hear the wild birds sing. I reached my hand to finger the dangling pendant on my choker as I recalled Weston's note to me. It didn't seem like an accident that his warning to remain true to my feral-bird self, rang so clearly right now. Shuddering, I tried to shake the image, but I had never felt more like a caged bird in my life, living in these fortress-like walls. My airway tightened with the need to see outside now more than ever. "I'm going to step outside for some air."

"Very well." Mavis stepped forward to finally leave me in my own privacy. "I'll be right back."

I took several heavy steps, each one drawing more strength from my core than the last, and before I could stop it, my knees buckled, and my mind went blank.

Moments later, Jon's voice boomed from somewhere in the room, announcing his arrival. "What happened?" His normal speaking tone carried the weight of his strength, but the way his words rumbled out this time, I felt them all the way into my bones.

"She's passed out," Mavis's voice wafted from somewhere above me.

A set of strong arms cradled me, lifting me up and placing me on my bed's soft surface. "Here's some smelling oil." Mavis's voice preceded pungent fumes of peppermint, and my lashes finally fluttered open.

My lips parted, but Jon quickly placed a finger on them. "Just rest." He shifted his gaze to Mavis. "She's pale as the linen. What has she eaten today?"

"I'm not sure. I had a tray delivered for lunch, but when I came back to retrieve it, it appeared she had only taken the tea."

Jon ran his hand over my forehead, and even though I had gotten used to the dryness of his broad palm, I didn't feel comfort. "She's very cold."

My vision was blurry, but I could see Mavis and Jon move around me, adding more blankets. "What's going on with this dress," Jon asked Mavis with obvious annoyance. "It's nearly hanging off her."

"That was worrisome to me too. She had her measurement taken for the dress only weeks ago, but it seems like she's lost a significant amount of weight."

I didn't enjoy the way they hovered over me, but I also didn't have the strength to insist I was fine. "Mavis, can you give us a moment. Perhaps call the doctor and bring her some fruit, or something else fresh." Jon's voice had turned soft and dithering, unlike any sound I'd heard. His gaze held onto her until the door was closed.

I didn't think it was possible for a face to be more concerned, but his lips descended another notch, and he looked me straight in the eye. "My dear, if I ask you what's wrong can you be honest with me?"

I forced a light shrug. "I must be tired."

"Of course, you're worn out. It looks like you haven't eaten in months. Your appearance has drastically changed since the first time I met you. Although I'm not complaining as you're still the most beautiful woman to me, I would be a fool to believe that you aren't suffering. It would behoove you to just be honest with me now. Are you heartsick about something?"

A small quiver shook my chest at the thought that he might be unhappy with this arrangement. I'd been doing everything I could to convince him—and myself—that this marriage was going to be fine, better than fine. Amazing. "I think it's the excitement of the wedding and all. Once it's all settled, I'm sure I'll feel stronger." As if to prove my point, I pressed my palms into the mattress and forced myself to a seated position.

The deep lines of his forehead creased all the way to his hairline. "I know you've been under stress, but I can't pretend I don't see what's happening."

My lips parted, but I didn't interrupt. His hand gently grabbed mine, and he brought it to his lips the way he always did, dropping a kiss on each finger and continued holding my hand in his. His gaze hovered on my hand for the longest moment, and he raised the most heart-stopping question. "Would you argue with me if I let you go?"

My eyes brimmed wide, and I rushed to stutter, "W-what do you mean?"

"If I said that I cared about you too much to watch you lose yourself in our marriage. I am willing to let you go, would you refuse?"

His words were lightning that shot adrenaline into my chest. "What—"

He cut me off, his words were so smooth and comforting, I knew he was genuine. "That war needed to end. I'm glad it's over and that I was able to help, but maybe our agreement can be sorted out another way. What do you think?" A worried brow pinched between his eyes as he regarded my face as if he was peeling away my secrets.

I *couldn't* reply. A yes would mean I lied to him, and a no would mean I was still lying. That slight quiver in my chest took it upon itself to swell four times bigger and rumbled around as if it had sprouted wings and was about to take flight. Being put on the spot like this wasn't fair.

I had done what was asked of me!

He lightly squeezed my hand, pressing, "There is something that's bothering you. I can't see what it is, but I have watched the spark in your eyes dwindle more each day, and I'm not going to lie to myself and say you are okay. So, if I'm not going to lie, I expect you not to lie."

I inhaled, trying to frame all my words in perfect context. I couldn't hint that I was ungrateful because he had done so much good. He had to know I tried. I didn't go into this unwillingly. I tried and I prayed, and I begged for this to work. No matter how hard I argued with my heart to believe this is what I wanted, my heart was just not hearing it.

There's no respectable way to tell someone you can't love them the way they love you.

This should have been stopped so much earlier, back when I was repulsed by him. It would have been so much easier then. Now, I'd seen what an honest man he was, and it made this so much harder, but he didn't deserve a wife who didn't love him. He deserved someone who loved him for . . . him. Tears welled in my eyes, as I connected my thoughts that brought me back to Reeves. My thoughts always brought me back to Reeves, and that simple plea he had for me. *Wait for someone who loves you for you.* Easier said than done. How long can people wait?

As I looked back at Jon, my gaze settled on fine gray strands of hair blended into his beard. They didn't make him unattractive, but told the truth of his age. Suddenly, I had a new thought. Jon was older, alone most of his life. *He settled for me.*

I licked my lips, bringing agility back to them, and sat up straighter. "Why did you pick me?"

Without even a flinch, he spoke in an even voice, "Dear, I've told you before, I was enamored with your spirit."

"You have told me that, but it's never really made sense to me."

"What is this about?" His gaze shifted around the room, as if he was looking for something to help clear up his confusion. "Do you not believe I'm sincere?"

"You are sincere." My voice was growing stronger as I saw so clearly where everything had gone wrong. This wasn't about the war, or Father, or even me. Something had gone wrong with him, not believing he could wait for the perfect person. He had to know I didn't love him the way he wanted. I never returned his kisses, and returned to my suite as soon as dinner was over, never requesting an extra moment with him. He's not stupid. "I'm going to be honest with you, and please don't pretend to be shocked, but we both know Ruenella was the better fit for you. She's quiet, and loves to read, dress up, and have fancy dinners. She's nothing like me, but everything like you. Why not her?"

"I've met plenty of Ruenellas in my life." He shook his head, physically rejecting the suggestions. "There's nothing wrong with them. Beautiful. Elegant. A bit of a romantic spirit." His gaze lowered to his hand still holding mine. His grip remained tender, not stiffening the slightest. "But that is where the issue lies. She yearns for romantic love. The kind filled with flowers, and all the things of novels. Often, that love is selfish." His eyes found mine, and were unwavering as he went on, "I could see right through you. You couldn't be fooled into that. Romantic love is not your thing. You are that rare person who is capable of unselfish love."

My brows beaded together, as I was deeply suspicious of his explanation. This was completely new to me. "How do you know that?"

He raised a brow up, deepening the lines on his forehead. "You didn't place conditions on anything. You gave up your life in your own country, to save your country." He held up a finger. "That's the truest love. If you have that, a couple can survive anything because the romantic love will die, and without the sacrificial love to take over, the bond of the couple will die as well."

He lifted my hand again, but this time my knuckle was shaking. He dropped one more kiss, letting his lips linger longer than usual before he placed my hand on my lap. "I'm not the monster you think I am. Perhaps in another lifetime, you could have loved me. But I can see this isn't about me. You are heartsick about *someone*." He blinked. He never deliberately blinks or fidgets when he speaks, but he blinked, and pulled up a tear. He'd always been affectionate with me, but never outwardly emotional. The tear had that knot lodged back in my throat so fast, I was gasping for air, and blinking back my own tears.

He took one step back, away from my bed, and whispered, "I love you enough to let you go."

Twenty-One
Reeves

Wearing jeans ripped in the knee the honest way, from hard work and long days, I hopped out of my tractor, and wiped the sweat that never receded off my neck. It was early spring, but a heat wave moved in, and I scrambled to get my sunflowers in.

I couldn't stand the sight of this field from my window. It reminded me of Erralee, and I refused to reminisce. After consulting with Weston, who really didn't seem to have much expertise in farming to weigh my decision, I filled the field with sunflower seeds with the goal of bringing color back to this spot. I think Weston's go ahead might have been more about me needing to move on, than grow anything that made money, but either way, the flowers got planted.

One thing I know, God has a funny sense of humor. When I planted this field, I started close to my house, trying to fill it in the most orderly way. Wouldn't you know it, I ran out of seed right when I got to the end—Erralee's spot. I could have easily gone to town and bought more seed, but God had another idea. He left me a perfect little dugout at the sunflowers' edge, and I wouldn't want it any other way. I can't see this spot from my house anymore, as the flowers camouflage it, but it's there if I ever need a good thinking spot.

I often thought about how I had tried to teach Erralee how to face her fears. My whole thing about when it's the scariest, that's when you jump. It's weird but now with hindsight, I think she was the one helping me, more than I had assisted her.

It's funny how I came to this small town, thinking war was the most inhumane thing a person could experience. I knew now God had sent me Erralee for a purpose. To teach me that no matter where I was in life, there was always more profound hurt. Someone always has it worse. That fact becomes a good reason to not dwell or get stuck on your own sorrows.

I didn't even have nightmares about the war anymore. Now, I struggled with my heartache of finding that perfect person I wasn't allowed to love.

That's a fact I'd never get over.

It wasn't fair.

I wasn't going to lie. I was tired.

It wasn't even exhaustion of my body. I'm getting my eight hours of sleep, actually sleeping better than I had in years, but this exhaustion was in my spirit.

I was tired of losing out, feeling the compression so hard in my chest.

I was tired of pushing.

It's not like I was giving up on life, or anything.

I was just mentally capped out.

It was a silent battle in my head, and I'd hidden it. Mostly because I stayed away from everyone.

If anyone knew how wrecked I was, they wouldn't want me around. Not that there's anywhere for me to go. There's no doctor on the planet that can cure what I had.

But I put my boots on every morning and poured my heart into my work.

Thankfully, the farming had never been better.

King D'Long had invited me to participate in a pilot program, which he finessed just for me. One where I was managing all the royal farmlands' crop rotation and was now on the payroll. Part of me wondered if it was Erralee's plan. The other part thought maybe he had guilt. Either way, it kept my mind busy, spending long days in the field.

With the extra money, I started a fund for a new barn for Hank. Next year, I'll add another horse, so Hank can have a companion. It wasn't much, but I learned I didn't need much.

The wind softened, twisting around me. DeJa'vu washed over me as I glanced toward the field. I blinked but failed to focus. My eyes knew her, but all I could hear was my heart pounding out, *I've found you*. My brain didn't even know what that meant. But my soul seemed to know what was happening. Erralee crossed my field, wearing a straw hat, jeans and boots. An oversized white button shirt hung over her jeans and blew in the wind. I blinked several times, waiting for the mirage to go away but it only came closer, and more into focus.

"Hey, cowboy," she called out, "I'm ready to work."

"Is that so?" I tilted my head, not quite sure of what game she was playing while still in disbelief over what I was seeing. "Well, you're in luck because I'm in need of some good help."

My heart pounded against my rib cage, warning me not to be fooled. Before I could check my words, I found them tumbling out, "Are you here with King Aswell?"

Without missing a beat, she nodded her understanding of my question. "No, I'm here for someone else."

My lips smashed together, steadying the tremble in my jaw. I wouldn't say my heart had hardened, but it had learned a lesson about letting people in. Her words dangled in the wind, as if they were testing me.

"I, ah, didn't get married." She looked at me with wounded eyes, but somewhere in the corner there was a glimmer that lit her expression with something I could only call hope.

I coaxed my head to the side, trying to hear that again. It was forward. Direct and didn't need an explanation. "Is that so?"

A joyless laugh sliced through the silence, and her voice unstable, cracking as it pitched higher. "I was scared. I thought I might miss out on a regular life."

My chin dipped, my body receding as I knew this was too good to be true. She came back to her field, because it was her field, it had nothing to do with me—

"And I hope it's not too late, but I was scared to miss out on a chance with you."

My brow bunched, my gaze fixed on her, seeking clarification. My heart rate picked up a notch as we both locked our gazes on each other. The connection that soared though my brain nearly buckled me.

"Erralee," I said, my words grating like stone on stone. I had started walking forward, but now I was nearly running, not stopping until I had her in an embrace.

"Am I too late?" Her voice crackled as if she was fearful for her life.

This wasn't a time for words.

I lifted her into a shoe-off-the-ground embrace, and Erralee's arms flung around my neck. She fell against me, and the coy smile that graced her lips pressed into my lips, the warmth of her skin on mine buckled my knees, completely *undoing me*.

Epilogue

My hand glided down the grand staircase banister rail as I kept my eyes glued to the doorway. *He was here!* I was able to jump down the steps, skipping every other one because I had slipped tennis shoes on under my dress, a compromise I made with Mother. I still wore the princess gowns for royal affairs, but in an effort to continue to practice making my own decisions, I refused to restrict myself to uncomfortable footwear. Mother and I adopted an out of sight, out of mind rule. If she couldn't see it, she couldn't make a rule about it. I committed to never letting a toe peep out from under my gowns. She committed to never pointing out how much shorter I had become.

I wouldn't say we've grown together. We also still don't really understand each other. However, we've formed a sort of mutual respect that I appreciated. Today, she and my whole family stood back against the great room wall, waiting for me to greet my guest first. I jumped the last two steps in one giant leap forward. So eager to get to the door first, I whipped it open without checking out the window to confirm who it was. I knew it was him!

Weston. Sweet Weston. His hair neatly trimmed, almost all the way to his scalp. My eyes practically bugged out of my head seeing him clean cut for the first time in his life. His eyes radiated all the emotions I felt thumping in my own chest. I didn't hesitate to fly into his arms, wrapping one arm around his neck as he bent down to hold me, and stretching the other hand up to rub his smooth head. "Where did your hair go?" I squealed out, my words falling into blissful giggles.

He playfully ducked away, removing my hand from his head, his lips in an open mouth smile. "Turns out I got used to it. I love not having it hanging in my eyes."

Still lingering in the astonishment of getting to hug Weston after so many nights of shedding tears of worry for him, I reached out to hug his neck again. This time, he didn't duck away, but lifted me up, and twirled me in a circle. We fell into a laughter spell reminiscent of our childhood giggles. When he nearly dropped me on my feet, I had happy tears in my eyes. "I'm sorry farming didn't work out but I'm so glad you are working at the palace again."

His shoulders rose all the way up and fell as he emitted an audible sigh. "Me too."

There was a pause as our eyes found each other's. "I have one request," I started slowly.

"I already know," he rushed out, tipping his head toward me. "You're upset I didn't tell you first."

"Yes!" My mouth dropped open, and my hand flew to my heart, as just the mere reference to his deployment made my heart twist. "Don't do that to me again!"

"Never." He was already shaking his head, physically shaming the past. "I understood how hard you would take it. I honestly knew you were going to be in safe hands. King Aswell has the strongest army, and you didn't need me."

"But you had to know, you're more than just my security guy." I reached out, touching his forearm gently. "You're my best friend."

"I know. And you are mine." He covered my hand and squeezed it for a mere moment before dropping it. He tore his gaze from mine, scanning the room. "Before this reunion turns into a sappy movie, let's do something fun."

"Fun?" I sputtered out, laughter seeding my breath again. "What did you have in mind?"

His gaze focused on the window, beyond the front yard. "Let's walk through the forest."

"That sounds like a good idea." As soon as the word was out, I pulled in a big yawn. "I'm about ready for my nap."

Hours later, I sat on a hollow log, half grown over with moss. Of course, I sat on the half that wasn't furry. Weston stretched out below me on his side in a pile of dead leaves, propping his head up with his hand. "Today was the best day," I said through a wistful sigh, one of the first comments spoken between us in the last ten minutes. We'd spent the whole afternoon, and early evening filling each other in on all the things we missed, and I can't believe it happened, but we'd finally run out of words for each other. "Are you glad to be home?"

"Definitely." His eyes shifted to a narrow side trail we hardly ever used in the spring. It was the one that would get covered in prickly weeds that scratched my ankles. "I am very grateful to be home . . ."

Hearing hesitation in his tone, my brows dipped down. "But?"

"It's not a 'but'," he rushed out, "It's a we have company."

"Company?" I checked behind me, following his gaze to the trail. Standing on the end of it was the person who made my heart melt. Reeves had his back leaned against a giant oak tree, arms crossed in front of him. He had on my favorite shirt, the blue one that matched his eyes. Both sleeves were rolled halfway up his forearm, revealing his all-year tan, and the end of his prosthetic. I found it funny how I no longer saw his prosthetic as a thing, it blended into the rest of his body. It was just who he was, and I loved him that way.

Just like I no longer saw us as two separate people from opposite worlds. I had argued with myself so much that one of the reasons we couldn't be together was because we lived two very different lives. It didn't take me long to see the fallacy in my prior thinking. Neither of us had to join the other person's life. Instead, we morphed together, creating our own world in the best way. He brought a somberness, and I held the free spirit. Together we blended perfectly, balanced. With a few minor discrepancies.

Maybe not a few.

One sort-of-an-issue thing.

I hated the sunflowers he planted in my field. I get it, it was a sentimental thing he did when he was trying not to think about me, and yes, it was epically sweet. But that was *my* field. I'd only ever known it to have wild grass with dandelions in the spring and way too much ragweed in the fall. I wasn't allergic to anything, so it didn't bother me. I loved the rolling prairie. So, other than the everyday bickerment we had about my field, we were a blissfully happy couple.

There was nobody on the planet who could make my heart pound the way it did just from the sight of him being near me. "How'd you find me?"

"Process of elimination." He strolled over the soft dirt, stopping in front of the log, and dropped to sit next to me. He wrapped his arms all the way around me, pulling me into a cozy side hug. "If you two are done," his gaze wafted to Weston before pacing back to me, "I have a surprise for you."

"Really." That piqued my interest, and I sat straight up, and jokingly waved to Weston. "You know I love you, right? But you need to go. I have a surprise."

Weston's lips spread into a wide grin, revealing his perfect row of teeth as he got up from the ground and brushed off his jeans. "I was waiting for it."

"What do you mean?" I arched my chin, peering up at him and then back to Reeves. "Does Weston know about it?"

"Let's just say." He waved his hand like he was wagering a bet. "I may have asked him to keep you distracted."

"For real?" Now, I was completely invested in whatever this surprise was, and I jumped to my feet. "Come on." I took a step toward the narrow path Reeves had arrived on. "What are you waiting for. Lead me to your surprise."

"Don't be so pushy." Reeves sprang up, and followed in tow, a full smile remaining on his face.

I turned to wave back to Weston, but he was already heading back on the trail to the palace. "When are you coming back?" I called.

"Reeves said two hours." His voice was already fading into the bushes.

"Oh, two hours." I tapped my chin, pretending to mull over the timeline. "What can we do in two hours? I'm not really in the mood to rock climb."

"No." He shook his head from his place near my side, as we strolled back through the path. "I don't think I'd want to do that today either. It's something else very special."

"You didn't plant more sunflowers in my field, did you?" My jaw dropped from that scary thought. "You know I wanted to keep it bare."

"It is about your spot." His lips pulled together tightly, sealing off any more words from slipping out, and my stomach dropped all the way down. I couldn't fathom why he didn't just automatically understand why I wanted this spot to be bare. After sunflower harvest, I begged him not to fill it back with seeds, but he never promised me he wouldn't. He said the price of flowers was decent, and it turned out to be one of the best investments he had made. The argument was always the same. I'd say, "I didn't care about the money." He'd say, "Of course, you don't. You're a princess." Then I'd quip back, "Yeah, a princess of a bankrupt country."

We'd go back and forth for several minutes, until usually we just decided to drop it. Part of me felt like he understood what that meant to me. The other part wasn't so sure because he would never promise me not to plant flowers there again. He wasn't exactly a stubborn person either. Every other thing we had a minor issue over, he usually gave in just to see me smile. My blood pressure started to race just from thinking about our land arguments. "If you are taking me to my spot just so you can show me your neat little rows of seeds you just planted, don't bother." I hmphed, and tucked my bottom lip in.

He looked over at me, shook his head, and returned to a neutral stance as we hiked the rest of the short trail. It was just getting dark, and the first few stars of the evening peeked out from a cloudless sky. The breeze hadn't even made an appearance today. It had been a long time since I had looked up at the night sky with ease and didn't have to pray not to see a flash of unnatural light, and flickers of bombs from neighboring towns. I wasn't sure if either one of us would ever get over that anxiety.

We slowed our steps as we gazed up at the effervescent stars. Reeves linked my hand into his and we crossed the path that led to my field. I tried to study the ground in the dim night light. It didn't look as if a tractor had driven over it recently. There were not even truck tire tracks in the soft spring earth. It was exactly how I had left it yesterday after my nap.

With my head to the ground, I kept searching the soil for signs of fresh movement, but there wasn't anything until we came over the last little hill, and I saw his truck parked next to my spot. My heart stopped.

Everything fell dead silent but my beating heart.

Reeves had created a romantic prairie picnic with a red and white checkered tablecloth lazily draped inside his pickup bed. White and red throw pillows were lined along the edges, perfectly placed to look as if they had just been tossed in. A lantern with a flameless candle glowed from the center, highlighting a covered snack tray and a stainless-steel wine bucket. It was easily the most romantic thing I had ever personally experienced. Although I wasn't one to swoon for all that romance stuff, just looking at it made my toes curl under.

"Come on." He pulled my hand, propelling me forward, but I didn't want to rush. Something inside of me called, demanding I slow my steps and take it all in. I inhaled the prairie-fresh air and flashed another look to the stars. Everything was beautiful, perfect and *peaceful*.

We stopped right by the open tailgate. Reeves paused, and I had assumed he was going to jump up and help me up too, but when he didn't move after a few moments, I turned to see what his deal was. He was looking at me with the sweetest expression. One that made all my insides melt, and my breath hitched in my chest. Suddenly I understood this wasn't about the picnic, as that wasn't my surprise.

Reeves had a ring. A simple gold band. It was the plainest piece of jewelry I'd ever seen, but it held all the power to make my gut swirl. We'd talked about this a little. I didn't really think he was serious, as we'd only been official for a month. Even though we both knew from our first kiss in this spot, I had no idea this would come so soon. We needed this moment to seal our commitment to each other.

But I was ready. Tears pricked my eyes as soon as Reeves dropped to one knee.

He held out the ring, pinched in his fingers, pulled his lips into that crooked smile I love, and said the words fairytales are made of, "Will you marry me?"

I didn't keep him waiting. My simple nod opened the floodgates, I flew into his arms. I couldn't wait to kiss him. Right before our lips met, I managed to whisper, "Yes. I will marry you."

I didn't have a single doubt that this was my perfect person.

He was someone who I loved more than anything.

He was the very person I had been *waiting* for.

He was someone who loved me for *me*.

Reeves broke our lip lock and showered little kisses up the side of my cheek as he created a trail to my neck. I relaxed, raising my chin and out of my peripheral vision, a cobalt bird I'd never seen before took off from his spot in the sunflower field and set off soaring higher and higher.

Quiet, and strong, he appeared to take his journey with determination as he flapped his wings until he was so high, he was but a mere speck before he disappeared into the muted sky.

The beaming smile I had momentarily swapped to one of contemplation as I saw it all too clearly as a symbol.

I had been caged bird before, living under Father's dynasty, but loving Reeves and choosing to marry the person *I loved* had finally set me free.

Dear Reader, Thank YOU for reading Royally Rugged. Guess what? Weston is getting his own book next! It's called Royally Guarded and is on track to be released early 2025.

Check out the preorder here: https://www.amazon.com /dp/B0D3JX9B6C

X.O. J.P.

Acknowledgements

It's funny how God works. He's brought a slew of people into my life to help me on this writing journey and often when it comes time to write down their names, I choke and accidentally leave people out.

I'm going to try to name a few because I definitely have a great team of supporters.

Here's my short list:

Thank you to Erralee for letting me use her beautiful name for this book.

My amazing editors – Brenda & Rebecca for this one.

Alt19 Designs – Thank you, Steph for slaying my cover.

My amazing family who never reads my books, but they tolerate me working on them all day.

My super readers, who read all my books early and polish up the finishing touches: Tabitha, Peg, and I added a new friend this time, Jane.

Brooks. I don't think you actually read this book, but you read all my others, and I'll give you a free pass because you deserve so much thanks.

ALL MY AMAZING READERS AND BOOK COMMUNITY! I couldn't do this without you. Well, I could but it wouldn't be as much fun. I get so much more from you guys—when you email and message me with your little comments and daily updates—than I could ever give to you with these books. I love the book community so much, and every day I appreciate having my little space in it.

Also by J.P. Sterling

Bosses and Billionaires Series (All Standalones)
Maid for my Billionaire Boss
Upcycling My Rig-Pig Boss
Kissed by My Billionaire Boss
Marooned with My Celebrity Boss

A Heart that Dances Series
Dancing on Broken Ankles
The Stars We See
A Heart that Dances
A Heart that Loves

Water and Stone Duet
Ruby in the Water
Lily in the Stone

Christmas Shenanigans (All Standalones)
Mingle All the Way
Tis the Season to Get Married

The Coffee Loft Series (All Standalones)
Pardon My French Press
No More Mr. Chia Guy (Coming Fall 2024)

www.ingramcontent.com/pod-product-compliance
Lightning Source LLC
Chambersburg PA
CBHW061528310726
48972CB00008B/2359